Synopsis

In 1852, Artemis Danger — a shy Irish
famine and grief — boards a vessel bound for New York,
seeking bread and breath in a new world. The sea,
however, is no gentle passage. A storm of biblical ferocity
tears the ship to splinters, leaving Artemis adrift in an
endless ocean, her survival balanced on hunger, will, and
salt water.

When she awakens on a foreign shore, she finds herself
in a land of cypress and shadow: Louisiana, where
swamps breathe like lungs and faith is twisted through
root and bone. Rescued — or captured — by a Vodou
priestess with designs of her own, Artemis must summon
a cunning she never knew she possessed. From captivity
to wilderness, from wilderness to the labyrinth of New
Orleans itself — a city of fever, of slavery's sorrow, of
masks and masquerades — she remakes herself by blood,
resilience, and fragile hope.

But New Orleans keeps its secrets. As Artemis carves
her place, she must reckon with the ghosts of the
drowned, the power of those who would bind her soul,
and the dangerous tenderness of a love that may not be
what it seems.

Salt & Cypress is a tale of survival and transformation,
where storm and swamp, ritual and ruin, collide — and a
woman forges her name against the tide.

Prologue

The sea was never meant to be kind...

It fed, it ferried, it buried. For centuries men called it mother, though it mothered no one. In its depths lay bones without coffins, prayers without echoes, and secrets heavier than anchors.

On the night Artemis Danger left Ireland, she thought the ocean would be her passage to mercy — a road away from hunger, toward a country where bread was not measured like gold. She could not yet know that the sea would take her measure first.

And the cypress trees, waiting on the far shore, would whisper her name as if they had always known she was coming.

Table of Contents

Chapter I - Departure

*"The beginning of all voyages is a leaving,
and leaving is a kind of death."*
— Anonymous sailor's log, 1847

The night before the ship set sail, Artemis Danger did not sleep.

Dublin's quayside was a hive of shadows: carts rattling under burlap sacks, dockhands bent like beasts of burden, women clutching shawls tight against the salt-laden wind. The ship, *Providence Star*, loomed above them, her hull black as a coffin, her sails furled like wings of a roosting bird. Artemis had never seen a vessel so immense. It seemed to her that one could vanish into its belly and never be spat out again.

She kept her hand upon the small parcel of bread wrapped in linen, her last gift from the soil of Ireland. Her mother had pressed it into her hand the night she died — three days before the fever took her entirely. The bread was hard now, stale and dry, but Artemis carried it as if it were relic or charm, a fragment of a vanished life.

Men shouted in English, in Irish, in tongues she did not know. A boarding list was read aloud, names swallowed by the wind. Her own — "Danger, Artemis" — was mispronounced, clipped and careless, but still her heart stuttered as if she were being called forward to judgement. She climbed the gangplank, her body trembling with hunger and cold, her eyes cast down to avoid the jeers of sailors who smelled of gin and salt.

The deck was a chaos of humanity. Families clustered with blankets and bundles, single men jostled for space, children whimpered as they clung to their mothers' skirts. Below deck, the air was already rank with bodies, lamp smoke, and the damp of seawater seeping into the wood. Hammocks swayed above rough-hewn planks where the poorest would sleep cheek by jowl, like fish in a barrel.

Artemis found a corner near a bulkhead and sat, her arms wrapped about her knees. She thought of home — though what was home now? A cottage with no roof, earth that yielded only rot, graves that multiplied faster than bread could rise. She thought of her brother, already gone to the fever, and her father who had vanished into the workhouse, his fate sealed in silence. Only she remained, a pale scrap of bone and will, cast adrift from all she had known.

The bell tolled. The sailors hauled lines, their voices raised in chant. Canvas unfurled above, catching the moonlight like ghostly wings. The *Providence Star* lurched, creaked, and began to move. The quay slid away, the cries of those left behind blending with the gulls' harsh laughter. Ireland receded, a dark smudge against the horizon.

Artemis pressed her palm to the ship's rough timber. She whispered a prayer — not to God, who had remained deaf these long years, but to the sea itself. She had been taught to fear it, to treat it as one might a capricious king: with reverence, with gifts, with terror. She prayed not for mercy — she had forgotten the taste of that word — but for endurance. Let the ship not crack. Let the bread not run out. Let her body hold fast.

Days bled into one another. The Atlantic stretched endless, a heaving desert of salt and foam. Sun blistered the deck by day; cold gnawed through wool and bone by night. The steerage passengers endured in silence, their talk dwindling as the bread dwindled, their gazes hollow as if fixed on worlds beyond this one.

Artemis learned quickly the lessons of survival. How to cradle her portion of porridge so not a grain was lost. How to drink sparingly from the barrel water that stank of iron. How to sleep curled against the bulkhead so the roll of the ship would not throw her. She listened more than she spoke, her shyness becoming shield, her silence a form of prayer.

There were whispers of storms ahead. The sailors spoke of "the great churn," of waters that swallowed whole fleets, of winds that could shear a mast like a twig. Artemis heard them and felt her chest tighten, though she did not show it. She had already seen what hunger could do to a land; what storm could do to a sea, she would learn soon enough.

On the seventh night, she climbed to the deck and leaned against the railing. The sea was black glass, stars spilling upon it like salt. The air smelled not of rot or smoke but of vastness, clean and sharp. For a moment, she felt the faintest stirring of something forgotten: awe.

And then the wind shifted. A sigh at first, then a shiver through the rigging. The sails strained, the ropes groaned. A sailor cursed softly, crossing himself as he spat into the waves. Artemis felt the deck quiver beneath her feet as though the ship, too, had heard the summons of the storm.

She held tighter to the railing. Ahead, the horizon was no longer smooth but bruised, mottled with clouds that climbed higher and higher like walls of ink. She thought of her mother's last words, whispered fever-thin: *The sea will claim you, girl. The land will keep you.*

Artemis pressed her forehead to the wood, the salt air stinging her eyes. Departure, she realized, was not an ending at all. It was the first taste of the test to come.

Chapter II – The Long Atlantic

"All crossings are bargains with a weathered god; coin is fear, change is faith."
— Fragment from a sailor's catechism, c. 1840

The days aboard the *Providence Star* arranged themselves like thin slices of hard bread: identical, brittle, difficult to swallow. Dawn meant the hatch rasped open, the rush of cold air, a bell's dull knell that made the ribs of the ship quiver as if it had its own heart. Men uncoiled from hammocks like rope; women sat up with blankets clutched at their throats, hair pinned quick by memory and guesswork in the dim; children blinked owlishly and searched the floor for crumbs of yesterday.

Artemis learned the ship by listening as much as seeing. Every plank complained in its own tongue. The pumps had a chorus. The great beam above her sleeping place ticked whenever seas built from the east. She could tell when the cook's temper soured by the way his ladle struck the cauldron; whether the cooper had been drinking by the slovenly roll of barrels as they were shifted for balance. A life reduced to senses became a kind of ledger. She meant to keep hers in the black.

A boy with ink-black lashes and a birthmark like a spilled tear beneath his eye began to hover near her— Michael, eight years if he was a day, who had boarded with an aunt that coughed into a rag and folded it deep in her skirt when she thought no one watched. Michael had the endless questions of children who do not yet understand the price of answers. Why does the sea breathe? How tall is America? Is it true men get buried in salt instead of dirt?

"It is true," Artemis told him once, low-voiced. "But they go over wrapped in linen. The sea has its own church."

He considered this gravely. "Does God attend it?"

"If He does, He stands at the back."

The aunt watched Artemis with a guarded look, as if kindness were a luxury that could not be afforded. On the second week she traded Artemis a sewing needle for two spoonful of porridge, and Artemis mended Michael's cuff. The boy held out his small arm with the solemnity of a knight being dressed for battle. Thread through cloth, knots against fray—Artemis felt the small power of fixing the world where it could be fixed.

Above deck, air was its own sacrament. She rationed it as carefully as water. The salt breeze scoured the stink of below and set a sting in her nostrils that made the world feel unbruised for a few minutes at a time. The sea was a wide grey back, the sky a lid fitted over it. Sometimes porpoises came like a travelling joke, sleek and insistent, carving laughter into the wake. Once a storm petrel skimmed the bows, a flick of ink on slate.

"Mother Carey's chickens," a sailor muttered, crossing himself. "Bad luck, that."

Artemis looked from the bird to his hands—brown, nicked, strong as knots. "How can a bird be bad luck?" she asked before she could stop herself.

The sailor glanced at her, surprised to find her voice. "You're Irish, aren't you?" His accent bent toward Cornwall. "You know better than to ask. Some things are spells because we name them so." He spat sideways, not

unkind. "Keep your eyes on the horizon, girl. It's easier on the gut."

She did. She learned the horizon: how it buckled under wind, how it drank colour from sky when rain was brewing, how it lay deceptively meek ahead of the worst blows. She watched the men reef sail and let it run; watched the captain—Jory Black—make a survey from the quarterdeck with a gaze neither hard nor soft, simply measuring. He was not a young man, but he was not old, either—his years were stored in the lines at his eyes rather than in his step. Artemis admired that: a body that did not broadcast the arithmetic of what it had survived.

They passed an American brig one afternoon, close enough to see faces pale as smears. Between ships, news travelled by arm and mouth. The brig shouted warning of a gale-line stitched southeast; the *Providence Star* shouted back thanks and a curse on insurers. The sea swallowed both sentences happily.

Below, the steerage became a market of small economies. A mother with a baby the size of a loaf traded lullabies for sips of water when her throat ran ragged. A widower carved saints out of scrap and exchanged them for bits of tallow to lengthen the guttering lamplight; his saints wore faces made of faith and despair in equal parts. A cardman with a singed eyebrow told fortunes for a twist of tobacco; he read from a pack so slick with use it had become a mirror for every dirty thumb. When Artemis walked by, he glanced up, and the side of his mouth twitched as if he saw both a profit and a trouble.

"Come, miss," he said one afternoon, "let me lay the ship for you."

"I've no coin to pay with." Artemis folded her hands into her sleeves. "Nor tobacco."

"Keep your smoke. A story will do."

She hesitated, then nodded once. He frowned at his cards, made a show of cutting, drew three like teeth.

"The first is the Tower," he said, though his deck had no pictures, only numbers and suits stained toward anonymity. "Crumbling and fire." He laid another. "The Moon. Lies and tides." Another. "The Queen of Cups. Drowning woman." He clicked his tongue. "But she does not drown."

Artemis looked at the worn pasteboards and saw only blank country. "You read what you'd like to sell," she said, and meant no harm by it.

The cardman's smile went thin. "I read what ships know. Some passengers court their fate; some hide under its skirts. You—" He paused, and for a moment his eyes sharpened. "You will learn to take without asking. That is not an insult. The world won't ask your leave when it takes from you."

That night she dreamed of trees she had never met. Their trunks rose from black water; their knees knuckled up like old men's joints. Draperies of gray hung from branch to branch as if the trees were speaking to one another through veils. In the dream the trees whispered her name. She woke with her heart snapping in her chest like wet kindling and Michael's small hand curled into her sleeve as if it had always belonged there.

On the tenth day, a funeral—if that is what one calls a body given to something that will not stop eating. The

infant's mother made no sound; her silence was a scream folded and folded until it fit inside her ribcage like contraband. Men took off their caps. A prayer bubbled up from somewhere and formed itself into words. The bundle slid over the rail and the sea took it with the indifference of a cashier. Artemis felt something in her stiffen like a brace of wood. Not cruelty; not resignation. A knowledge. Names had weight only on land. Here, one was reduced to pulse.

Toward evening a glitter found the rigging—cat's hair of light feathering the ropes and the tips of the spars. St. Elmo's fire, the sailors said, low, as one names the dead. The air smelled of iron filings, penny-bright and bitter. The captain set more hands to the pumps, and the cooper hammered staves with the concentration of a man arguing with his own coffin. The sea lay down deceptively calm, a cat belly-up to be stroked. Even the children fell hush.

"Gale coming out of the south-southeast," the Cornish sailor told Artemis without looking at her, as if talking to himself. "Feels like it's loaned from someplace with a better claim to it."

"Loaned?"

"It'll collect." He blew air between his teeth. "The sky's a scales-pan; we're the coin rattling in it."

Artemis tried to keep her tasks unchanged as the weather changed. She washed her rag. She pinched her cheeks before going on deck, a vanity that felt like an argument with emptiness. She bartered her needlework where she could—tightened a hem, mended a cap—stored away scraps of fats for the worst days. But every

small deed swam in a tank with larger, stranger fish. The ship's voice lowered; the pumps spoke more often; the captain's steps grew clipped. The cook tied down his pots with a sailor's knot as if he expected the kitchen to leap.

The afternoon before the storm's blunt fist found them, Captain Jory Black came among the steerage with the ship's doctor, a round man with winter-green eyes and a cautious mouth. The captain's hat would not sit right; the wind tugged at brims as a child tugs a sleeve. He spoke plain—no reason to spend more words than the weather would.

"We reef at dusk," he said. "After that, no one above unless called or carried. You'll think the worst thing is the sound; it isn't. The worst thing is panic. Panic gets a body drowned in three feet of water."

His gaze caught Artemis for the smallest blink, then moved on. She felt seen in a way that made her spine correct itself. The doctor handed down little parcels of powdered bark to those coughing; to the aunt with the rag-hemmed cough, two, and a warning to keep her away from the babies. Disease loved a crowd, loved a hold; it was another passenger who had not paid.

Wind unstitched the day in long seams. The sky bled from pewter to ink. When the order came, it came as a chorus; the men swarmed the rigging, furled and kissed canvas to spar with hands that had been taught another alphabet long ago and now had to read fast. The sea rose, not dramatically but with that slow, brutal intention of a man standing up from a chair to deliver a blow.

Artemis held Michael's shoulder as the deck canted and the world lurched into two positions: this angle, and that. Buckets went skidding; a barrel thumped and was wrestled into submission by three men as if they were calming an ox. Light thinned to grease, then went out. The lamplight below flexed and flared, flexed and flared. The ship spoke in bone-voices.

"Tell me a thing that is true," Michael demanded suddenly, his voice small but flinty, as if he had been saving the question for exactly this minute.

Artemis thought of Ireland's fields that had yielded black hunger for three straight years. Thought of her mother's hands, cracked as winter. Thought of a priest who had told them God tested those He loved. Thought of her father's back as he went into the workhouse stumble-legged beneath the shame of living.

"That the sea ends," she said. "It does end. On a shore."

He considered this, then nodded once, solemn as a magistrate. "And after shore?"

"Trees," she said before she knew why. Her throat tightened. "Tall ones. With bells of grey hanging from them. They say your name without mouths."

Even below, night had weather. It pressed and withdrew. Wood sang. Nails complained. The aunt coughed until her ribs rattled like loose cutlery. Somewhere someone began to recite the beads, not expecting the prayers to be heard, only wanting the voice. When sleep came it flew in jagged wings and landed badly.

At dawn the horizon vanished.

There was no line between sea and sky—only a white that was not the white of linen or milk or bone but the white of noise, a colour that existed only where things broke. Rain came sideways hard enough to sting skin numb. When Artemis tried to look into it, the world blurred to streaks. She held to the bulkhead and felt the ship's ribs punch and recoil as if taking blows.

"Below!" a voice roared. "Below with you!" A sailor—young, mouth cut like a careless slice in a loaf—shoved her and three others toward the hatch, not cruelly, only with the inevitability of law. She slid down the slick ladder and into the smell of wet wool, tallow smoke, and human fear.

The hold swelled with sound. Babies shrieked as if the air had teeth. A woman prayed in Gaelic, the words as old as peat. A bottle rolled; someone lunged, caught it, swore; someone laughed, that high glassy laugh people make when the only alternative is to bite through their own tongues. The cardman, hair plastered, grinned at Artemis with eyes that had too much light in them.

"Tower and Moon," he shouted to her over the din. "You remember? It's the Queen keeps her head."

"What does she do?" Artemis called back before she could stop herself, her voice grainy with fear and salt.

"Counts," he said, and tapped his temple. "She counts the beats. She counts the breaths. She counts the ways a door may be closed and opened."

The ship dropped, and for a second everyone rose from the floor, a brief prayer of weightlessness. Then it climbed, and people slammed back into their small

earthly lives. The pumps slammed like fists. Water sloshed and retreated. Michael's hand found Artemis's again, as if guided.

Hours distorted to rope—knot by knot, moment by moment, her mind learned to move along them without looking down. She learned the tilt you must adopt to make a body into ballast. She learned the rhythm of the long heave and the short, sharp slap. She learned to hold her breath not in her chest but in the narrow place behind her breastbone, a shelf of air set aside for emergency. She learned the luxury of swallowing nothing but spit and staying alive.

Once the hatch burst, flung open by a careless wave or a hurried hand, and the white of outside poured down like a wild thing. Men yanked it shut again; a rope was thrown around its handle and tied so quickly Artemis could not admire the knots in time to understand them. She felt a rough calm settle inside her, the calm of a woman whose fear had spent itself and now moved through her like weather through reeds.

She remembered the captain's voice: Panic is the enemy. She said it inside her head the way children suck peppermint to feel brave.

Night came again. Or perhaps it did not; time was water and had no edges you could grip. The ship threw itself against the sea and the sea returned the favour. Somewhere above, men shouted to other men in the shrinking vocabulary of survival. Below, humanity slept in fits and starts, used up, too tired to be terrified for every minute available. Artemis did not sleep. She counted—beats, breaths, the seconds between the pump's long exhalations, the number of rosary beads the praying

woman got through before she started again. Counting made a line across the chaos. She walked it.

Toward what might have been dawn again, the ship straightened in a way that was worse than the heaving had been. Stillness announced itself like a stranger in a dark room. The pumps slowed. A silence fell so suddenly some people began to cry from the absence of noise.

Then a blow landed—solid, sick, unmistakable. Wood shouted. The hold tilted hard to starboard and stayed there, as if the sea had taken the ship by the jaw. Screams rose, layered and human and helpless. Artemis felt the tilt travel through her bones and fix there like a new rule of anatomy. A child slid; she grabbed his collar; he yelped and clutched at her. Water—cold and shockingly unnegotiable—came in under the hatch with a cat's paw first, then a hand, then two hands.

"Strike! Strike!" someone bellowed overhead. "Rig's gone! Hands to—"

The voice cut as if severed.

Artemis's mouth filled with the taste of pennies. She thought, very calmly: *This is the part where one thing decides the next hundred things.* She could not name the one thing yet. She only knew it would not be screaming.

She set her back against the beam and planted her boots, made herself into furniture. Michael latched on like a barnacle. The aunt coughed and coughed; the sound was a metronome; the metronome faltered; the metronome went on. A man began to sing in a thin, high voice about a girl who sold rings in Galway. The song faltered on the line about the rings. The ship groaned. Something heavy and metal skittered near their feet and went away.

Above, the sea took a breath and decided to hold it.

Artemis Danger, who had been more quiet than earth, gathered herself toward the next minute the way a diver gathers toward the jump. Her hands were raw; her knuckles had learned the ship so well they might as well have been married to it. She counted—one, two, three—and waited for the door to open, the water to come, the world to choose.

It would. It always did.

And she would choose back.

"Hope is a thin rope; learn your knots."

Chapter III - A Gathering Of Storms

"When the glass falls, count your breaths.
When it shatters, count your dead."
— Saying among North Atlantic pilots, c. 1830

The ship had learned a new grammar. It no longer spoke in the long, patient vowels of travel but in consonants that cracked and bit—*slap, slam, snap*—as if the sea were spelling its anger against the hull. Artemis measured the minutes by these sounds. The pumps wrote their blunt syllables: *work-work, live-live,* an incantation rude and necessary as bread.

Above, the storm took possession of time. Below, the steerage clung to pieces of it like drift. People slept because their bodies betrayed them; they woke to a taste of iron and the ache of having been gripped by fear for too long. Artemis held the boy Michael to her side and felt the smallness of his bones through wet cloth. The aunt coughed into her skirt until the cough seemed to own her mouth. When the fit broke she whispered an apology no one had asked for, as if shame were also a passenger taking up scarce air.

A hand-lantern swung on its hook, painting a hooded light over faces that had been cleansed of anything nonessential: all ornament rinsed away, leaving only fear, stubbornness, and the odd, flaring humour that people carry even into dark water. The cardman's hair lay slick on his scalp; the singed eyebrow looked newly minted. He had tied his deck into a little oilskin bundle and worn it at his throat like a saint's bone.

"Queen keeps her head," he muttered to Artemis when the ship staggered and then steadied, undone and done again in the same breath. "You remember? Count."

"I am," she said, and found she was. One, two, three—she counted the pump strokes, the breaths between the aunt's racking coughs, the time it took for fear to crest and ebb inside the ribs.

From above: a voice like a bell hammered by wind. "Strike the main tops'l! Hands aloft!" Then another voice, lower, clipped. Captain Jory Black, she thought, though words were chewed by distance and storm. "Heave to! Bear off that canvas! You there—mind the leach line!"

The ship answered with a deep complaint as men rose into the rigging to reef the sails, their bodies turned to black runes against a sky that wanted no witness. The *Providence Star* was no vast emigrant palace, only a working hull with ambitions; still, her masts loomed as if they had grown from an older forest and remembered the wind of that first world. They groaned now with the effort of being trees again.

Artemis had promised herself she would not seek the sight of the storm. She would stay where the wood and the breathing and the counting were. But then a barrel broke loose—poorly chocked, unlucky; it thumped toward a knot of women with that indecent glee things acquire when they become deadly. She rose without thinking, planted her bare feet, and shoved. The rim hit her shin and pain sparked white, but the barrel checked, wedged against a beam. A sailor dropped through the hatch, skidding and cursing. His hair was plastered to his skull; a tiny lightning seemed to creep over it in blue-

green threads, the ghost of St. Elmo's fire still fingering him.

"You'll have that leg for a souvenir," he barked, shoving the barrel into a corner and lashing it twice-fast. She recognized his voice then—the Cornishman who crossed himself at petrels and taught her the horizon. He glanced at her shin. "Wrap it tight. Blood's for carrying souls, not painting decks."

"Take the boy?" she asked, already knowing the answer.

"Not where I'm headed." There was no pride in it, only fact. He hooked a coil of rope over his shoulder. "Counting?" he asked, quick as a blessing already spent.

"Yes."

"Keep to it." He vanished up the ladder as if yanked by some invisible line.

The doctor came after, round and wet and worrying his lower lip with his teeth. He pressed a strip of linen to Artemis's shin, tied it with hands made clumsy by cold. "You'll have a half-moon scar," he said, voice pitched low so panic would not hear it and come closer. "Consider it a navigational mark."

It would have been a joke if the ship had not shuddered then, hard enough that the lamp smashed and snuffed. In darkness, every mouth opened large enough to swallow the room. For a heartbeat Artemis felt time slip; the counting vanished; the world had the blankness of a wall.

Then another lantern flared, the wick kissed alive by a flint-strike. Light returned in its mean ration. She drew air into her chest like rope into a coil. One, two, three.

A shout from above turned men into messengers. "Mizzen's carried! Cut away!" The words came down the ladder with a rain of spray.

"God help them," someone whispered.

"God keeps different hours at sea," the cardman said, a kindness wrapped in cruelty, or the other way around.

The next blow was a sound more than a movement— wood tearing in a long, wet rasp, like a tree dragged over stone. The ship lurched as if relieved of a limb. A cheer went up—half triumph, half grief—for cutting a mast is a kind of amputation that means life if done at the right time. The cheer shred to silence as another sea hit, shorter and meaner, a punch to the flank.

The hatch yanked open and three bodies were spilled down with the water: two upright, one not. The upright ones were all hands and rope and orders, dragging the third by his arms. They laid him in the narrow valley the deck made toward starboard. His mouth opened and closed; his eyes were dizzy clocks. Blood threaded from his ear as if some small fisherman inside were hauling out line.

"Mate's down," one of the sailors panted. "Block took him. Where's the bloody leech— Doc!"

The round doctor was already there, his face candle-pale. "Hold him," he ordered. He pressed fingers to the man's scalp, the ear, the hollow at the throat where pulse bargained. His mouth went a patient line, the way men's

mouths do when they have practiced bad news. "He breathes," he said. "For now."

Artemis eased forward, made herself useful. Linen. Water if there were any that was not salt. A hand to steady the lantern. The man's hand found hers blindly, squeezed with a sailor's grip that expected rope to answer. She squeezed back. Out of nowhere, an image: a tree with a grey beard, its knees up out of black water. Artemis blinked it away. The dream's voice was too near. Not yet, she told whatever it was that whispered. Not yet.

"Hold the lad," someone called. "Girl—Irish—hold the lad!" A child—a different child, not Michael—was being passed over heads in that urgent, casual way people move bread or buckets. Artemis reached and took him, felt his breath flutter like a bird caught in a palm. He smelled of tallow and terror.

Michael's hand found her leg and remained there, proprietary, calm. She looked down and saw the set of his small jaw. He was learning too much too quickly, the way all storm-children do.

Water began to seep, careful and insinuating, through the seams at the hatch. Not the great blows in buckets that the sea liked to throw when it amused her; this was a lawyer's water, making its case patiently along the boards. The ship answered with a slow, steady roll as the pumps kept up their argument.

"Above," a voice barked—this one very surely Captain Jory Black's. "Twenty hands. You—no, not him—he's spent. You. And you. Bo'sun, fetch me that spare tackle. We'll ride her head to. If she'll let us."

Artemis surprised herself by moving toward the ladder. The decision rose in her like a fish, without the help of thought: go. She shoved the child back into his mother's arms, pressed Michael's knuckles once. "Count," she said to him, the way you tell a sentry his duty. His eyes told her he would.

At the foot of the ladder the doctor caught her sleeve. "Orders are to keep below," he said.

"My hands know knots," she lied, because knowing how to learn is the next best thing to knowing. He stared for one heartbeat, then let her go. He did not have time to own anyone's fate but his patients'.

Wind greeted her by taking her breath and flinging it away. The deck was a slick sentence made of verbs. Rain came not in drops but in lengths of rope. The sky was a lid of unlit pewter; the sea was a book whose pages kept tearing themselves out. Around her bodies moved with the extravagance of desperation—the particular grace men adopt when death is both audience and partner.

"Back below!" someone roared, seeing the thinness of her. She ignored him, as a woman ignores a wind she cannot afford to acknowledge. She found the Cornishman's back and stuck to it as if it were the leeward side of a tree. "Take this," he shouted without turning, thrusting a line into her hands. "Bowline. Rabbit comes out of the hole, round the tree, back in the hole. Make a queen of it. Quick now—quick!"

Her fingers learned in a breath what they needed to know. The bowline snugged; the line held. The Cornishman risked a glance, and something like

approval cut through the rain. "You'll do," he said. "Mind your feet. The deck's shopping for fools."

A wave rose up like a wall decided to travel. The ship climbed it, slid down it, climbed again. Over the starboard rail a shape blundered—a spar still married to rigging—battering the hull with the malice of wreckage. Men swarmed it, knives in fists that looked made for prayer, sawing, swearing. Artemis leaned her weight into a line and felt, with a shock like recognition, the answer of the ship in her bones. She was ballast and brace now, at least for this minute. She could not be more than that; she did not need to be.

"Mind that fouled sheet!" someone howled. "Haul, for your mothers' sakes!"

They hauled. The ship eased her head to wind, not docile but momentarily persuaded. Relief came like a cheap drink—fast, hot, treacherous. The captain stalked the quarterdeck, rope in hand, hat gone, hair sluiced flat. He was soaked to the skin and looked made of tar and determination. He glanced across the chaos, found Artemis for a sliver of a second, and did not waste the breath to send her below. She had bought her minute; he had other accounts.

Lightning unrolled across the sky in a strip so near the light had sound. For an instant the world was a copper engraving: men etched black against a white that hurt; ropes like strings on a huge, unreasonable instrument; the sea showing all its teeth at once. In that flat fierce illumination Artemis saw, miles to windward, a darker darkness within the dark—the line of something not-weather. She did not know enough to name it. The Cornishman did.

"Lee shore," he said, and the words had the weight of a verdict. "Christ save us."

She looked at him and saw the peculiar poverty of that prayer at sea. Land was not mercy in a storm; land was the knife held steady while you ran at it. Waves break their backs on shoal and rock, and after that they break ships.

"Compass is mad," another sailor yelled. "She's been set all damned day."

"We'll wear ship," the captain shouted. "If the rudder listens." He did not bother to order God about. He did not have that habit.

The rudder answered as if drunk and insulted. The wheel jerked; men threw their weight. The ship hesitated, an old horse asked to climb a hill it remembers breaking a leg on. A sea hit her abeam and she skated sideways, canted, considered submitting. Then the bow found a sliver of better water and took it. The captain bared his teeth, which was as near to a smile as a man gets while bargaining with a storm. "Hold her," he growled, to the wheel and to fate.

Another blow to the hull—this one like a fist with rings. Something gave. Water came over the waist of the ship with the ferocity of a mob, slamming bodies to knees, scooping tools and hopes off the deck. Artemis's hands tore free; the line burned her palms. For one blank instant she was no one's daughter, no one's name, only a mouth in water. Then the Cornishman's arm hooked her belt and yanked with a competence that had been bought dear long ago. They went to their knees together and then to their feet—if what they made could be called feet at all on a floor that refused to be floor.

"Below with you," he shouted, voice raw. "You've bought your look. Go."

She went because he had saved her, and a debt like that asks obedience. The ladder was a waterfall. She plunged down through it, into the stink and breath and human heat as if diving into a different weather. Michael's face flashed up out of the dim like a coin from the bottom of a pocket. She crouched and put her mouth to his ear.

"Still counting?"

"I lost sixteen," he said, furious with himself. "I had seventy-two, and then I had fifty-six."

"Then begin again," she said. "We are allowed."

The cardman sat with his knees drawn up, cards under his tongue to keep them dry by some logic of faith. He spat them into his hand, shuffled idly, though the pasteboards made only a wet whisper. "Land," he said to Artemis, voice low. "I saw it when the lid lifted. We are being herded to it like pigs to a fence."

"Is there fence enough for all?" Artemis asked before she could help herself.

He smiled without teeth. "Always."

The pumps slowed once—just once—and the room went very still, like a child listening for the next scold. Then they resumed. A woman laughed a little and clapped her hand over her mouth, shocked by herself. The doctor worked at the mate's scalp with a needle and thread, the man's chest rising with bellows-strokes that had nothing

to do with sleep. Blood ran in thin pinks where rain caught it and diluted it on the boards.

Artemis tore a hem from her shift and bound her palms. The skin had raised in little coins where the rope had kissed it hard. She did not feel the pain now; it would come later, like a tax. She took the aunt's hand without asking. The woman seemed not to notice until the fit ended and she found her fingers captured.

"I'll die of this," she said, matter-of-fact, like a woman admitting a debt.

"Not today," Artemis said. It was not comfort; it was inventory.

The ship fell—no, not fell: stepped into absence, as if a stair had been removed. Bodies rose. A crucifix leapt from a nail and skittered. A baby wailed as if insulted by gravity's failure. The ship hit bottom—if what she hit could be called bottom—and everything that could rattle did. Somewhere far forward a sound of grinding spoke in a new voice: stone flirting with wood. It lasted only a heartbeat and then was gone, but the echo wrote itself on every face within the lantern's sway.

"Breakers," someone whispered who had grown up on a coast. "Sweet Mother."

The word travelled the hold like a rat, seen and not, leaving small screams in its wake. Breakers meant a mouth of white water that bit and bit again; it meant a lee shore where the storm pushes you at exactly the wrong speed—fast enough to destroy you, slow enough that you have time to know it.

Orders from above, brief and rimed with fury: "Hands to the longboat—No!—stand off that—belay, I said! Pump, you bastards, pump as if you had mothers! Bo'sun—sound the well!" The captain's voice had a finality that let no man pretend. He would not allow the farce of a boat in these seas; he would not pretend salvation came in easily stowed packages.

Michael's hand climbed her arm to her throat. "After shore," he said, as if finishing a lesson they had begun long ago, "trees?"

"Yes," she said. She did not know where the certainty came from, only that it stood as if on pilings. "Tall ones. With grey bells."

His breathing steadied as if the image itself were oxygen. The aunt watched them with the hollow patience of the exhausted. The cardman began, without meaning to be cruel, to sing under his breath, and others took the tune, and then the language left and all that remained was a round thing made of sound—no words, only the promise of words, which is sometimes better.

Artemis closed her eyes and let the song move through her like a slow river. She counted it without counting: the way it swelled and ebbed, the way it remembered something no one had taught it. Perhaps storm had its own hymn. Perhaps bones did.

The pumps laboured. The ship negotiated. The storm gathered itself, not to end but to improve. There is a point in all weather where intent reveals itself; even rain has its character. This gale had decided it wanted to be a story men would tell with their backs against tavern walls, gesturing with scars. It wanted to write itself on hands

and houses. It wanted, most of all, to have the land to help with the killing.

Another silence, the kind that is actually sound—the hush of too much water arranged in the wrong directions. A single voice from above, not shouting now but near: the captain at the hatch, lantern behind him making a small halo that mocked him. His face was open in the way men's faces open when they are done spending lies.

"Listen," he said. The word carried without force.

They did. The roar was not the roar of wind or rain or the long tearing sigh of a ship defying being broken. It was a crowd's roar, thousands of small mouths making one large hunger. Artemis had never heard surf at night on a coast like this, but she knew it as a creature knows another creature.

"We'll try to wear her into deeper water," Captain Jory Black said. "If she'll mind her helm." He looked at them—at Artemis, at Michael, at the cardman, at all the faces that had become fewer and identical—and gave them what truth he had left. "If not—" He stopped. He was not a man for conditional tenses. "Hold to one another," he said, and was gone.

He had not told them to pray. He had not told them not to. In his omission there was a kind of grace larger than any sacrament could manage down here.

Artemis kissed the tips of her fingers—a gesture she had learned from her mother when bread had been handed through a window by a stranger—and pressed those fingers to the beam above her head. It was not a superstition so much as a signature: *I was here. I touched this. We made a promise.*

The promise was small. She would keep the boy's counting alive. She would keep her hands useful. She would not make a noise that stole anyone else's breath. In the end of worlds, small vows hold.

Above, the wheel shrieked again. The ship decided, or was decided for. She turned, unwilling and magnificent in her refusal. For a moment Artemis felt the change as a shift in her blood, a new groove laid down. The roar altered its pitch by a fraction; the deck's angle eased from one impossible to another merely unreasonable.

"Good girl," the Cornishman's voice came, spent and fierce. He was speaking to the ship. Men speak to women and ships in exactly the same tone when life and death are at stake: command made of love, love made of command.

The reprieve lasted as long as a rosary bead rolled under a boot. Then a wave found them broader than was safe, set its shoulder, and shoved. The hull slid sideways; the grinding returned, closer this time, a flirt become an assault. Wood screamed—a sound that undoes a human mind because it should not exist. Somewhere forward something opened that should not open. Water entered as if invited.

"Sound the well!" a man bawled, voice breaking. "For—" and then his words were a cough, and then the cough was water, and above it all the storm said its one word again and again: *Mine.*

Artemis pulled Michael tight into the lee of her body. The aunt's hand crawled up Artemis's sleeve and stayed there, small as a child's. The cardman, with a neatness that would have been comic if anything were funny now, tucked his cards back into the oilskin and tied the thong with fingers that trembled only a little.

"We will need wood," the doctor said to no one and everyone. "And cloth. And a place to lay the broken."

As if the world heard him and wished to be generous, the ship heaved and something heavy fell with a concussive thud—the long-boat, perhaps, jostled in its chocks. Men swore with conversant eloquence. The storm laughed with its lungs full.

Artemis did not pray. She did not dare interrupt the business of surviving with a conversation she half-believed in. She counted. She kept the boy's breath steady by matching it. She placed her hand—raw, bandaged, transient—against the beam and felt the ship's shiver pass through wood into bone and back again, as if the two of them had shared a body once and remembered it.

The gathering was complete now. Storm had invited all its cousins: wind with nails, water with judgment, land with appetite. The feast had begun.

And somewhere ahead, past the roar and the white and the blind maps men make when they close their eyes and pretend, they can see, the breakers lifted their many heads and waited.

"A lee shore is land pretending to be mercy."

Chapter IV - The Breaker's Maw

"When land comes in teeth, choose water."
— Old pilot's axiom, origin disputed

The roar changed. It was no longer the roar of sky and rain and the long bellow of a labouring hull; it was crowd-noise, thousands of small mouths making one hunger. Even below decks the sound arranged the air into a warning. Men stopped speaking in whole sentences. Women fixed blankets that would not stay fixed. Children lifted their heads like animals scenting fire.

"Breakers," someone said, and the word crawled around the hold like a live thing.

The captain's lantern appeared at the hatch. A wet halo cut him down to the bone of purpose. "We'll wear her into deeper water," he said, voice pitched low and even, the voice of a man who had learned the alphabet of panic and elected another tongue. "If she minds her helm." He did not say *if not*. He had the sense to keep conditionals out of a room where breath was already scarce.

The pumps spoke their blunt prayer: *work-work, live-live.* Artemis pressed her palm to the beam, feeling the ship's shudder travel bone to wood and back. She counted with the pump: one, two, three. Michael's small fingers climbed her sleeve to her collar, a creeping vine. The aunt coughed until the cough owned her mouth and

then, as if shamed by its excess, retreated. The cardman tucked his oilskin into his shirtfront like a talisman and looked at Artemis through rain-slick lashes.

"Queen keeps her head," he said, soft, to remind her not of hope but of the posture required in its absence.

A blow like a fist with rings struck the hull. The deck kicked. Somewhere forward a grinding flirted with the timbers and then withdrew. Men cursed eloquently above, the captain answering with orders cut down to one breath apiece. "Bear her off! Brace the fore! No—belay that—sound the well!"

"Feet of water in the bilge," came the bo'sun's voice, strangled by wind. "More in the next minute than the last."

"Then make the next minute worth the water," the captain said. "Heave."

The rudder answered as if insulted. The ship hesitated, an old horse at the memory of a bad hill—then, with an effort that hurt to hear, she turned. The roar altered by a hair; the deck's angle eased from impossible to merely unreasonable. A cheer began in one throat and died there, strangled by the next wave.

Artemis did not know she was moving until she felt cold fire on her face—the rain that lives outside. She had climbed into the storm without intending to, legs making decisions ahead of her mind. The deck was a sentence made entirely of verbs. Ropes ran like snakes, clever and dangerous; blocks swung with the malice of wreckage. The wind snatched breath and flung it overboard to save weight.

"Back below!" a sailor bellowed, seeing the thinness of her. She ignored the command as a woman ignores weather she cannot afford to respect. The Cornishman was a dark knot against the pale—she found the lee of his body and held to it as if it were a tree. He thrust a line into her hands without turning.

"Bowline," he shouted. "Rabbit out the hole, round the tree, back in. Make it queen-quick."

Her fingers learned by theft, swift and unashamed. The bowline bit and held. He risked a glance; approval flickered. "You'll do. Mind your feet. The deck's shopping for fools."

The compass lamp guttered. Lightning unrolled and for an instant the world flattened to copper: men etched like woodcuts against a white that hurt, the sea showing all its teeth at once. In the engraving Artemis saw, far to windward, a darkness within the dark—no cliff she could name, exactly, but the fur of something like land. The Cornishman saw it and did not let his mouth change shape.

"Lee shore," he said into the rain. "Christ save us."

Land, in storm, is knife. Waves break their backs on it. Ships follow.

"Wear her!" Captain Jory Black's voice, raw and absolute. "If the helm will hear. Stand by the fore—haul—haul, damn you—"

They hauled. For a breath the bow found kinder water and took it. Relief came like cheap whiskey—hot, fast, treacherous. Then a sea shoved broadside and the hull skated. Wood screamed. The grinding returned,

intimate now, as if stone and plank had been introduced and found each other suitable.

"Longboat?" someone yelled.

"Belay that nonsense," the captain snapped. "You'll launch a coffin."

Another sea boarded the waist. Artemis's hands tore free; the line burned her palms into small round coins. The world became water. Up had no content. Down was a rumour. Her mouth filled with the taste of pennies and tar, the old marriage of rope and labour. A hand took her belt—iron-competent—and dragged her out of the blankness. She coughed up half a breath and spat the other half. The Cornishman's face hovered at her shoulder, the eyes of a man who had spent all his jokes long ago and saved only the good ones.

"Below," he said, and because he had saved her, she obeyed.

The ladder was a waterfall. She dropped down it, into heat and stink and human fear, a different weather. Michael's eyes flashed coin-bright; his hand found hers and stayed, proprietary and relieved. "Counting?" she asked.

"I lost them," he confessed, furious. "I had seventy-two and then it was fifty-six again."

"Then begin," she said. "We are permitted." She wiped hair and rain from his face with a tenderness that surprised her by being present, fully, in the middle of everything.

The hatch burst. Men spilled down with water as if poured. Two upright, one not. They laid the not-upright man in the starboard valley the tilted deck made. The doctor hunkered, winter-green eyes narrowed to work. "Hold him," he ordered. "You, girl—lantern."

Artemis steadied the light. The mate's ear bled thinly. His chest climbed and fell like a bellows that did not believe in itself. The doctor's needle flashed. Thread stitched scalp to skin, skin to the stubborn idea of staying.

The pumps slowed once and the silence that followed was monstrous. Then they resumed. Someone laughed once and clapped her hand over her mouth, scandalized by the crime of having found a laugh in inventory this poor.

"Girl," a woman whispered. It took Artemis a beat to locate the mouth. The aunt had two dry spots on her cheeks where tears ought to have been. "Take the boy," she said, as if giving away bread.

"I have him," Artemis said. "We'll have you, too."

A new blow answered that lie on her behalf. The hull juddered and the room tilted as if on a hinge. Water knuckled under the hatch, careful at first, then bolder. The cardman stuffed his cards back under his tongue like sacrament.

"Hold to one another," the captain called through the hatch, not sermon but instruction. "If she goes, let her go. Take wood that floats. Don't lash. Do you hear me? Don't lash."

Don't tie yourself to a sinking argument. The advice had other uses. Artemis grabbed for rope anyway—habit is older than wisdom—and then dropped it, trusting a stranger's rule with the faith of the desperate.

A scream that was not a voice at all, but wood being wrong. The deck lifted—no, was lifted—and they were all momentarily saints, feet not touching earth. Something heavy fell and a new passage opened forward where no passage belonged. The sea came in, catlike first, then dog-mean, then as sovereign. It hurled bodies against beams with the democracy of force.

Artemis's hand got Michael, then lost him, then got him again, fingers cramped to claw around his wrist. The aunt slid—the hold had become a tilted city—and struck a beam, breath knocked from her like a word stolen. Artemis lunged, caught cloth, felt it tear.

"Go," the aunt mouthed, coughing up nothing. "Take him."

"We take you," Artemis said, and reached again. Another sea came and thought made no difference. The beam between them filled with water. The aunt's hand lifted in a small, formal gesture—farewell or blessing, it was hard to know—and she was gone among legs and blankets and crates and water that wanted everything.

Michael's mouth opened; sound did not. Artemis put her face to his and shouted where only the two of them could hear. "We float," she said. "We float *now.*"

The hatch heaved. For a heartbeat the storm itself stood in the doorway, white and without edges. Men with knives in their mouths and rope over their shoulders

slammed it shut; a lashing crossed and held. The pumps
bellowed. The doctor swore in a language that did not
require a priest.

Something cracked in the ship's spine. The sound had a
grammar: past tense becoming present. The longboat
tore loose—Artemis saw it in her mind if not with her
eyes—and came skidding, then took another set of men
like a hand scooping grain. The deck leapt, paused as if
deciding whether to be deck any longer, and then chose
elsewhere to be.

The world became pieces.

Artemis's body found air and then water and then air
again all in the space of a heartbeat. She slammed her
shoulder and learned a new word for pain. Michael
vanished—not by intention; boys do not vanish on
purpose—but because the sea is a tyrant of custody. She
clawed at the water with both hands and found only rope
that wanted to marry her ankle, a plank that wanted to
bruise her, and a silence where a small hand had been.

"Michael!" The word left her mouth like a bird that does
not know where land is. Her eyes were full of salt and
lamp-smoke and grief. She dove once, twice—she had
breath for three dives, she decided, and used two of
them to find pain and wood and hair that might not be
hair. On the third her fingers met something soft—no
child—and the sea rammed her upward with the patience
of a bouncer escorting someone out.

The captain's order lived inside her head: *Take wood
that floats. Don't lash.* A hatch-cover bumped her
shoulder, generous as a door. She threw her weight
across it and felt it consider her like a horse considers a

rider: Will I? Will I not? It bore her. She hooked one leg, then the other, and locked her arms until they burned.

The Cornishman's face surfaced a fathom away, hair plastered flat, eyes bright with the unmistakable energy of a man who has one more thing to do. He flung a small shape toward her—oilskin wrapped and tied. "Knife," he shouted, or "life;" the storm stole the consonant. The bundle smacked her forearm. She trapped it under her body and made a knot of herself and the hatch.

He lifted a hand—not farewell, not blessing, simply a mark on a ledger: *done.* Then a spar swung out of the night with the slow decisiveness of a judge's hammer and took him under in a clean stroke. The water showed her nothing after that except its white intention. She waited for his head. The world declined.

A new shape lurched closer—the cardman, pale as church wax, his mouth open around words that had been evicted. He had his oilskin at his throat like a saint's bone. He saw Artemis see it and took it off and flung it. It fell short; she swam off her door to catch it and the sea deprived them both with the charity of a magistrate. When she turned back to her hatch, it had spun a quarter-turn and was already beginning to think of leaving.

"Float," she told it, which was absurd. "Float with me."

It did. She hauled herself up, chest to plank, legs scissoring under the skin of the world. The hatch teetered, dipped, and rose. She lied to herself in a voice calibrated exactly for lying: *My blood is warm. I know east from west. Boys float like corks.*

Up had a colour: not white, not grey, but the colour of broken things. Down had a sound like summer gravel poured out of a sack. Time took off its edges. She remembered to count. One, two, three—breaths, or heartbeats, or the moments between waves that offered a look at the sky.

Pieces went past: a barrel with its hoops blinking like rings; a crucifix on its nail; a woman's shoe that would never be a pair again. A man clung to a ladder and called a name; the sea corrected him. A boy's cap spun like a small planet and then sank quickly, as if someone had cut its tether.

Artemis called once—"Michael!"—and got back her own voice, thinner. The sea returned nothing. She tested the word *boy* inside her and found it hurt too much to move.

Night went on being the same kind of night. The storm did not so much slacken as change character, each wave a cousin, new and intimate, interested in her specifically. She made bargains. She would let a wave have her left leg if it would leave her hands; she would offer a memory in exchange for one more float. Her mind brought up her mother's bread wrapped in linen, stale as a relic; her father stepping into the workhouse with his head down; her brother coughing through the night like a tenant who would not be evicted. Things to put down on the scale. The sea weighed them and smiled with all its teeth.

Wind leaned back a little. Rain came less like rope, more like pins. The hatch settled into its work. Artemis learned its language quickly: how to roll into it rather than against it, how to let hips and knees become hinges,

how to make her body into a brace instead of a sail. She thought of the cardman's silly catechism—Tower, Moon, Queen—and laughed once, a single bubble, at the indecency of surviving long enough to get the joke.

When lightning flared the world arranged itself into stark ledger lines. In one of those strobed instants she saw, far off, the ghost of the *Providence Star*—a broken alphabet of mast and rigging and men still arguing with their own deaths. Then the sheet of illumination rolled away and left only the afterimage smouldering in her eyes.

The oilskin bundle the Cornishman had flung pressed its corners into her ribs. She found the knot with her teeth, worked it, spat salt. Inside: a palm-knife, short and mean, and a second skin of canvas that might one day be a sail, and a corked vial of something smelling of tar and turpentine—lamp oil. Tools, not salvation. She slid the knife into the bodice of her dress and told herself this was what queens did: held edges where the world came apart.

Toward what passed for dawn, the sky did not lighten so much as change its refusal. The roar quieted by degrees. The white became grey. The grey acquired shapes. Waves were no longer a single will but many, competing. The hatch rose and fell in a smaller arithmetic. Artemis watched her breath make a cloud and scatter. Her teeth had a conversation of their own.

Bodies floated. She catalogued them because counting was how she stayed inside the wall of herself. Not many. Not few. Enough to make the sea feel like a crowded room where no one would meet your eye. She did not look for faces. She had learned one lesson perfectly

overnight: there are things you only survive by not naming.

A gull came, uninvited and unashamed, riding the new day as if it had invented it. It spoke the gull's single word: *me*. Artemis hated it for being correct and envied it for the honesty. It circled twice, decided she was worth no curiosity that could not be answered by the smell of rot, and went away to better prospects.

The wind backed. The sea took longer to organize injury. A swell lifted her and she saw the world as a line of low shoulders and no land at all. The breakers' voice had vanished—either behind her or nowhere near her to begin with. The ship's last argument with stone had flung its pieces wide and her farther than anyone could have selected on purpose.

She spoke aloud because the silence wanted to make a nest in her throat. "We are permitted to begin again," she said, and did not expect an answer.

Her hands had lost their feeling sometime in the last hour; this felt like mercy until she tried to adjust her position and learned there are worse things than pain. She blew into her fingers and found she was making a gesture her mother had taught her—warm your hands before asking them hard work. She could not remember the last time she had worked them at anything as simple as dough.

A dark edge skated under the hatch. She froze. The edge returned, closer—sleek as a curved blade, conversationally slow. The fin cut water with the politeness of a man removing his hat before an

execution. A second fin quarrelled with the first, then decided to keep company.

Artemis drew her knees up, made herself narrow, and pretended to be made entirely of wood. The sharks were ideas with mouths. They tried the hatch with their bodies and teeth, discovered it had no fat, and rolled away, interested in another argument. The sea is lavish in its entertainments.

She did not cry. She did not have water for the luxury. Rage rose and passed like heat-lightning. Beneath it lay something quieter, older: the same stubbornness that had kept the pump speaking, *work-work, live-live,* all through the worst. She had not asked to be saved. She had asked to be counted. The sea had obliged in its peculiar way.

The sky brightened until it could be called day by someone with a forgiving tongue. The wind went to sulk elsewhere. Waves still had teeth but were no longer planning a meal. Artemis lay on her hatch and tried to inventory herself like a ship's manifest: one body, scraped and bruised; one knife; one piece of wood; one mind that had not yet decided to quit; one handful of names she could not afford to say.

Somewhere, out beyond this circle, trees lifted grey beards of veil and whispered her name. She had never stood among them, not in waking life, but the dream came and stood beside her like a sister and refused to go. *The sea ends,* she had promised the boy. It did. On a shore. She had proof only in the muscle of belief, but belief is a muscle, and she flexed it.

She hooked the canvas under her chest and over the hatch to make a poor man's awning. It flapped and tore a little and then learned its work. The oil she kept corked—lamp oil does not quench thirst; it teaches a lesson the body cannot unlearn. She counted the minutes it took for the sun to come out from behind a moving wall, counted the shadows cast by waves like the hands of a busted clock.

Afternoon—or what she named afternoon—arrived, and with it a sickly quiet that had danger hidden in it. Silence at sea is never silence; it is merely the absence of something you have grown used to. Artemis accepted it with suspicion. A loose board bumped her hatch and she caught it with one numb hand and wedged it crosswise to widen her raft's argument with gravity. A better float. Not a boat. Words matter, but not to water.

She slept. Or rather, she closed her eyes and arranged her breathing into something that fooled the part of the brain that keeps watch. When she woke, light had shifted and her skin had been salted dry in patches. Thirst had taken off its gloves and begun its work.

"Begin," she whispered, because there was no other verb available. "Begin again."

Night came back, tender as a bruise. Stars appeared by ones and twos until the whole black was salted with them. She could not tell whether the shipwreck had moved away or she had; motion is another of the sea's jokes. Far off—so far she could not have claimed it on any map—a faint line made itself visible, black against blacker, the merest stitch between sky and world. It might have been land. It might have been cloud. It might have been a lie.

She ate belief anyway. It was the only ration to hand.

The hatch rocked. The knife lay warm against her sternum, a secret spine. The whales of sleep rose and fell under her; she stepped from back to back and kept her balance with the same small vows that had held the hold together: do not steal breath, do not spend noise, count.

When morning came she would be the last of the *Providence Star* unless the sea contradicted her. If land waited, it waited in a language she did not yet speak. If not, she would learn the names of thirst and sun and naps of death. Either way, she had already done the thing that teaches you how to do the next thing: she had chosen back.

The breakers had wanted an ending. She, perversely, had selected a beginning.

"Float first, Pray after"

Chapter V – Afloat Among The Dead

"Count your breaths. Wet your lips with rain only.
Salt is a liar."
— Marginalia in a ship's prayerbook, water-stained,
author unknown

Dawn arrived as a bruise learns to fade: by slow degrees,
never all at once. The sea, which had spent the night as a
mob, woke with the hangdog quiet of a thing that had
enjoyed itself too much. The waves still had teeth, but
they were no longer planning a meal. Gull cries stitched
the air in coarse thread. Clouds trailed ragged hems.

Artemis lay upon the hatch and did not move until her
mind returned from wherever it had fled in the last
hours. When it came back it came in pieces: hands that
ached and did not feel; a shoulder that had learned a
new alphabet of pain; the weight of a knife warmed by
her own sternum; the faint oily tang rising from the
bundle jammed under her ribs. Her mouth was a kiln.
Her tongue found cracks along her lips and read them
like roads to nowhere.

She lifted her head a little. The hatch scissored under
her, undecided, then steadied as she learned again its
language: hip with it, not against it; knees loose; one arm
threaded through a crosspiece. The canvas she had
thrown over the slats in the dark—more hope than plan—
hung from two corners, limp and cobwebbed with salt. It
had licked up dew at some hour of night. She squeezed
the cloth hard over her mouth. Three reluctant drops,
not enough to call water, struck her tongue. They were

so sweet she could have wept if she had anything left to spend.

"Count," she told herself, because that habit was the rope between moments. One, two, three—breaths at first. Then gulls. Then the rhythm of the hatch. The counting made a wall; she stood behind it.

Bodies kept her company. Some floated face down; some bellied to the light; some held bits of ship the way children cling to toys that will not save them. The sea did not arrange them kindly or cruelly, only to its convenience. A woman's shawl had wrapped itself around a spar; the shawl moved as if it breathed. A man gripped a barrel with his arms cinched tight as rope; he would not let it go and it would not keep him. A rosary trailed from a wrist, beads black as wet seeds.

Artemis did not look for the faces she feared to find. She had learned a perfect lesson: survival is sometimes only the refusal to name what floats near you.

A fin incised the surface two strokes from her hatch. Then another, and another. They moved like polite knives, circling a little as if they were reading a menu. One brushed the hatch with its side. The touch was impersonal and terrifying, like bureaucracy. Artemis drew her knees up and made herself thin, wood and cloth and bone packed tight, a parcel beneath notice. She slid the knife out an inch because the sword you cannot see does not exist, and then slid it back because the sword you show is a conversation you may not want to have.

A barrel drifted within reach and she trapped its rim with the arch of her foot, sheeting the canvas over both to widen the raft. The lashings the captain had forbidden were not these lashings; she used strips torn from her skirt, double-knotted with a washerwoman's stubbornness. The hatch accepted its new companion with a small groan and floated better under her, as if pleased to be part of a plural.

A voice came across the water. Not a shout—there was no spare air for shouting—but a reach.

"Help," it said. A man's voice, scraped down to one syllable.

Artemis jerked her head toward the sound and regretted it as pain set up a forge in her neck. She eased and scanned, careful. There: a ladder section, tilted like the page of an open book, and upon it a man whose hair lay flat as a seal's. One of his hands had been unmade by something with a mouth. He used the other to paddle toward her with a weak doggedness that made a case for him in a court she did not remember convening.

Between them, three fins corrected course, interested. If she moved toward him she would pour the scent of her small life into the water like a sentence. If she did not—If she did not—

He did not call again. He dragged the ladder an arm's length and stopped. The sharks made small, practical decisions. The water threshed, then quieted. A patch of pink ribboned away in the wake. The ladder righted and went on alone, humbly.

Artemis did not add a number to the tally she kept in her head. Some arithmetic is not for speaking aloud. She

swallowed the pebble of her shame and felt it lodge under her breastbone where grief keeps a shelf.

Hours gathered. The sun climbed and became interrogator. Thirst put on boots. Skin that had met salt and wind and fear all night began to break down like old linen. The canvas awning gave poor shade but some, and every scrap of mercy mattered. She turned in small increments to keep what skin she could from the worst of the light, because dignity is sometimes math.

The little vial of oil—tar-scented, made for lamps and ropes—tapped her ribs with suggestion. Sailors said oil could calm troubled water. In fair seas it could; a sheen would quiet a chop, round the heads off small waves. This was not fair sea; but the water at the hatch's edge slapped and slopped in a way that jerked the little shelter loose. She wet her thumb, smeared a stingy ribbon across the surface. The water answered with a melt at the rim; the slap softened. It was not miracle. It was one degree less of punishment. She let herself be proud for exactly one breath, then went back to counting.

Toward what she chose to call midday she smelled something that was not sea. Not land yet. Something vegetative, a green taste in the nose. The storm had dragged them far. She could not know how far; men with compasses and charts might not know. But smell is a map too. She licked her lip and tasted nothing but salt and blood. Still: the other fragrance persisted, shy as a guest at the edge of a crowd.

A short squall shouldered across the bright, threw two curtains of rain, and left. She spread the canvas wide, gulped with her mouth open, let water strike her tongue and her eyes and the cracked lines across her mouth.

She caught a handful of it in the hollow of the hatch, washed quick—salt off skin first, salt out of cloth second, salt out of hair if there were any left for vanity. She wrung water into her palm and sipped in measured swallows, tasting the metallic gift of pennies turned to sweetness. Her belly, offended by medicine after famine, clenched and then unclenched. She held it down by imagining bread she had eaten years ago, thin and blessed, and the work of kneading that had warmed her wrists.

A long shape rose and fell beside her in silence. For one lunatic breath she thought whale—salvation recast as a fairy tale—until it rolled and showed a white belly scribbled with scars. Dolphin. A pair. They kept to her beam for a minute, peering with the disconcerting appraisal of intelligent animals. She forbade herself to invent meaning. Still, when they slid off into another business, she felt lonelier than she had the instant before, and the loneliness had teeth.

The dead travelled too. The sea arranged them into tempers: those that bobbed, those that sank and returned, those that became sentences cut off mid-word. A child's hand bumped the hatch; the wrist had lost the idea of a body. Artemis made a sound without meaning and lifted her elbow to let the hand go by without snagging. The cloud of flies that would come later was still far off. She would not drink that future until it arrived.

At some hour—afternoon, perhaps, though the sun was everywhere at once—she saw the cardman. He floated face up, mouth open, as if considering a story. The oilskin thong was still at his neck; the leather had shrunk to a hungry line. She sculled toward him with precise

strokes of one hand, made a hook of her finger, and snagged the thong. The card-packet slid free with the indifferent ease of a thing no longer defended. The sharks, busy elsewhere, ignored her theft this once.

She lifted the oilskin onto the hatch and set it flat. The knot had welded itself. She did not open it. It was not a deck anymore. It was a reliquary.

"Queen keeps her head," she told him, as one speaks to the changed. "Thank you for the lesson."

When she pushed him away, he turned slowly, as if surprised, and went on contemplating the sky. She used both hands to wash her own face and hands with rain caught in the oilskin's seam; this was the indulgence of ritual, no more. She let it stand.

The light sharpened. Shadows drew clean edges. Heat worked at her, in her, through her, like a tailor intent on making the world fit her to its purposes. She tucked her burned hands into the cool fold at her sides. She imagined snow falling on the Connemara hills the year her brother had gone, the lacework on the pub window, the smell of wet wool. Memory is a drink with no effect but comfort.

The sea, having tired of courtesies, threw a different lesson. A dark bar drifted into view at the edge of her trivial horizon—wood, thick as two men together. Two bodies had trapped themselves there with ambition: they had lashed belts across chest and plank. One was already not a man; the head hung backward like a blessing gone wrong. The other, still in the somewhere-between, lifted a hand when waves allowed. His palm flashed white as a gull's belly.

The captain's instruction lived in her: *Don't lash.* She had obeyed because she had not had a length of rope and because she had believed him. Now, watching the belt-bitten flesh, she believed him twice. Still, she reached out in the small form of her reach—two fingers crooked, will flung over water—and whispered, "I am sorry," though the men could not hear and the sea would not care. The bar slid by, purposeful, wanting no witness.

She thought of the aunt with the cough and the little boy she had promised to keep in numbers. She thought of the Cornishman with lightning in his hair and a competence that had made breathing seem like a job one could keep. She worked one stake out of the hatch and did not ask whether the ache in her throat was thirst or a name bitten back.

By late light the world gentled in colour but not in fact. The long, slow heave of the sea rather than the short, mean chop; the wind lower, as if embarrassed by what it had wanted before. A slick of weed fingered past—wrack, with crabs that had made a traveling city of it. Perched upon the tangle, thin-legged and irritable, a bird with a spear-bill and a monk's hood watched her. Tern? She had no words for the families of birds in this hemisphere. It stepped twice, judged her a poor genre, and lifted in one clean beat of wing.

When night lay down upon the water it did it with a kindness the day had not. Stars salted the black. She could see for yards, not miles, but the seeing soothed. Waves made the old grammar: rise, hesitate, fall. She bound her palms again with a cleaner strip torn from the hem and sang not a song but the scaffolding of a song— no words, only the cradle of a tune. It was the melody

her mother had used when kneading: stretch, fold, turn; stretch, fold, turn; give the dough and the day their share of your warmth. The note did not carry; it did not need to. It occupied the air within her mouth and made something soft there.

Cold arrived late and demanded rent. She paid with shivers. They had no rhythm she could use. She burrowed her cheek against the hatch, drew her knees up, lay close to the oilskin parcel for its dense, indifferent heat. Sleep came in slippery fish. She caught one, two, lost the third. She dreamed of trees rising from water with grey beards of veils and knees like old men's joints. The trees did not make promises. They repeated her name in a way that made it seem older than she was.

She woke to a sound more felt than heard: the hush of a great flatness ahead. The sea around her remained restless; but somewhere in front it grew quieter, as if kneeling to be blessed. She lifted, craned. The hatch tipped obligingly. A line existed that had not existed before—only a shade darker than the darkness. Between two stars, a seam where the world might split.

"Shore," she said, not convinced by evidence but by the need to say the word out loud.

By morning the line had thickened and broken into low humps, then into hummocks with darker studs—the idea of trees. The air changed. It carried up from the world ahead a smell she had never known and knew at once: rot and bloom braided; mud with authority; leaf-sweat. The smell of a place that made things and unmade them in the same hour. She did not know the word cypress. She knew the word *keep*.

Birds multiplied. Not the clean, cameo cries of open sea-gulls but a chattering as if a crowd had gathered on purpose. The water's colour shifted from hammered tin to the slick brown of tea left too long to steep. Freshwater bled into it in secrets. Artemis dipped a cupped hand, touched it to her mouth, and tasted a lie so sweet she almost believed it. It was less salt, not no salt; it flirted and then refused. She spat, smiling at the trick of it.

Tide? River? She was too small to name the currents that gripped her hatch and adopted it. She felt herself gathered and set upon a long slide that did not care who she was, only that she did not fight harder than she could afford. The barrel knocked her hip; she knocked it back like an apology. The oilskin thumped. Somewhere in her chest the piece of shame that the man on the ladder had left lodged turned over and settled; it would live there now, weathering with the seasons.

A shape travelled under the hatch with lazy menace. Not a shark—broader, with a back like a blunt hill. It sighed. The breath rose in a bubble that kissed her thigh and popped. She flinched, then laughed, a dry sound. The beast—manatee, though she did not know the name—bumped the barrel, considered this new fact, and moved on with the majestic unconcern of a thing that does not have to justify its preferences. She did not ask for its blessing. She accepted its indifference.

The first palisade of breakers took her with a practical kindness. They did not cream white; they did not wheel her under. They shouldered the hatch, lifted, carried a space, set down. The second row had less courtesy. They slid under, then above, then under, and her hatch

forgot for three heartbeats how to be floor. She held, hip, knee, arm through slat, knife a hard truth against her chest. The barrel dragged, wrestled the lashings, then decided—wisely—to remain. She told it *good* under her breath, as if it could be praised into obedience.

The water lost depth by inches. The colour kept the colour of tea and grew crowded with sticks and leaves and pollen and things that had been parts of other things. A seedpod knocked her knuckle. Insects arrived, then corrected themselves and went back to their own concerns. The air possessed her; it was a hand. She breathed, she coughed, she breathed again.

She saw land in the old way for the first time in her life: not cliff or town or blessed harbour, but a low, patient smear studded with green. The trees wore grey lace. Their knees rose out of the shallows like men hiding beneath tables. Birds stood upon them, absurd as punctuation. The word in her mind was not *home* and not *mercy*. The word was *answer*.

She felt safe enough, foolishly, to take inventory aloud the way a woman will in a kitchen when she means to work from scraps. "One hatch," she said hoarsely. "One barrel. One knife. One canvas. One—" She paused and looked at the oilskin. "One deck of cards, perhaps. One woman. One body. One name."

She thought of that name as something that could be set down and taken up again like a tool cleaned with oil. *Artemis Danger.* It had sounded like a taunt on the quay; here it had the shape of a vow.

The last reach of water—no longer sea, not yet river— tricked them. It made room and then withdrew it. It offered a channel and then threw a log across it. Her hatch stuck and shivered free. Her shoulder put its case strongly, and the barrel, loyal out of habit, aided. Mud rose in slick creatures beneath. A root like a drowned finger stroked her calf and she hissed, then apologized to the root for the hiss.

She did not try to land. Land will take you whether you try or not when it means to. She held the hatch the way a person holds the last sentence of a prayer they do not believe: firmly, stubbornly, in case they are wrong. The trees approached without moving. Veils hung from their arms, grey and indecent. The air had the temperature of skin. Flies auditioned her. A fish threw itself at afternoon because afternoon had offended it.

A boat moved among the knees of the trees: not a big boat—a dugout, its man standing at the back with a pole. He wore a hat brimmed against the light and his skin flickered water-brown. He did not see her, or saw her and mistrusted the sight. He pushed on and was gone in noise like nothing but its own.

She set her mouth and did the only right thing left: nothing. The current made the day's last argument and won. The hatch lifted over a low lip and slid into a pocket of slack water so sudden and private it made a sound like a sigh. The barrel settled with a hollow cluck. Bugs approved. Leaves arranged themselves where leaves like to be.

Artemis let go.

Her hands did not understand the order and held anyway. She spoke to them like disobedient children. "Enough," she said. "Enough now."

They heard and obeyed.

She fell sideways into water warm as breath. It took her without remembering who she was, which may be the kindest way water can take you. Mud came up like a second pillow. The last thing she knew before the black gathered was the fringe of a grey veil swaying above her like a bell pull, and the shape of a bird stepping sideways upon a knee of wood as if gossiping.

"The sea ends," she informed the roots, because she had promised the boy and promises require witnesses. "On a shore."

She did not know if the roots believed her. She did not stay to argue.

"When the sea refuses your name, let the trees pronounce it."

Chapter VI - Ashore

*"Where salt ends, rot begins,
and both are a kind of hunger."*
— From a mariner's commonplace book, 1849

The world returned as sound before it learned to be
sight. A busy buzzing braided with drip and slow suck; a
frog sounding the same low syllable over and over as if
tallying debts; a wing's soft scissor by her ear. Artemis lay
with her cheek in warm mud and her mouth open to
water the colour of old tea. Her body belonged to
someone else—heavy, unwilling, badly harnessed—and
she had to call each limb by name before it remembered
being hers.

The veil above her was not cloth but growth: long grey
beards of it, moving with a breath the trees made. The
air pressed, damp as hands. She lifted her head an inch;
pain flashed in a clean stripe from collar to skull and
then subsided to a thrum. The hatch had wedged itself
half into reeds and half into the low lip of root that had
held it like a mother who meant well. The barrel
knocked faintly, patient, as if to remind her of the
bargains they had struck.

She had not died, or if she had she had come to a place
that smelled of leaf-sweat and old wood rather than any
heaven she had been promised. Her tongue found
cracks in her lips and read them like roads. She rolled,
slow as season, slid an arm through a slat, and drew the
canvas back over herself with a motion learned in the
night—hip with it, not against it; knees loose; make a

brace of your body and the world will sometimes agree to keep you.

Counting returned as a rope caught in her hand: the frog's call, the drip, the small skein of insects sawing the hot. One—two—three— The numbers were not truth; they were rails to run upon.

A ribbon of water braided past her ear from the canvas's hem. She sucked at it and got a quarter mouthful, copper-sweet, so miraculous that for a breath she could have wept if there had been anything left to spend. She sat up inches, then an inch more, and the world unfurled: trunks rising from water; knees like old men's joints; roots knuckled into the shallows; green dark as an under-dress; veils everywhere, greyed with age and weather and some other thing that felt like intention. Birds stood upon knees as if gossiping; one was all white, needle-beaked and annoyed, looks pinched as a matron's.

She was ashore, though the ground wore water the way a poor woman wears jewellery on Sundays—plainly, because there is no other. She tried the word *land* and it stuck to the roof of her mouth like a sacrament too dry to swallow.

The knife lay warm against her sternum where she had tucked it before the world broke. The oilskin bundle waited by her ribs. She touched both with the reverence fear teaches. Her hands had become strangers—swollen, grated, turned into maps of small hurts—and the act of touching made her know them again.

Between two roots the water deepened to a shadow. Something moved there with a lazy authority that made

no promises about its preferences. A back like a low hill turned, sank, forgot her. She thought of all the names she did not know for the citizens of this place and decided to keep her ignorance quiet inside her teeth.

"Begin," she told herself, because the word had kept its usefulness. She pushed the hatch a hand's breadth higher on its root, let the barrel help, set the canvas so it made a sulk of shade over her head. The air went from unbearable to merely intimate. She breathed it as one breathes in a small room where a woman is kneading bread—warmth with work in it.

Insects arrived to audition her. They bit, inspected, revised their judgments, returned with cousins. She slapped once, twice; then remembered there is more to be lost by fighting a city than by living quietly in its neighbourhood. She tucked her burned hands into the cool seam at her sides and studied what mattered.

The small bundle the Cornishman had flung at her in the night—the mean palm-knife, the square of canvas, the vial smelling of tar—was inventory and shrine. She set it near the root where the water licked but would not quite reach. The other oilskin—the cardman's deck—she kept at her hip without opening, because some reliquaries are more useful unopened.

A snake passed three feet off: thick as a wrist, the colour of silt, mouth closed, uninterested. Artemis held her breath with both hands and let it write itself off the page. When it was gone she let breath go and found herself trembling—not from that brief possibility of teeth, but because the tremor needed somewhere to sleep and she had offered it bone.

Across the slow water a shape resolved and then did not, being both boat and not-boat until her eye learned the grammar of this place. A carved thing, low as a sentence whispered—dugout, long as four men—came on a thread of channel between the trees. A man stood at the stern with a pole as if he were walking on the water's back. His hat had a brim like a puddle turned upside down. Behind him, under the grey veils, a darker shade moved with the boat's own patience.

They were quiet when they came. The man's pole slid and rose, slid and rose. The other shape at first seemed second man, then seemed bundle, then seemed woman: a figure upright but hooded, wrapped not in mourning but in purpose. She wore indigo faded to a good history and a headwrap the colour of a crow's wing wet with rain. When they were ten yards off she raised one hand and the man stopped the boat as if the gesture had caught the water by its collar.

"Eh bien," said the woman—not a question, exactly, but an address. She did not speak like the quay in Dublin; she spoke like a place where a river learns its mind. Her eyes were the colour of wet bark and did the work of two hands. "La mer spit you out, tres chèr?"

Artemis made to answer and coughed instead. Her throat had been salted to leather. She nodded because the neck could manage nods and not much else.

"Don't move," the woman said, but the command was gentle, woven through with the common sense of someone who had watched more than one creature tear itself by hurrying. She made a sign across her breast that had as much to do with habit as belief; then she reached down into a basket and brought up a bottle with a paper

label the colour of old bone. She shook a little of it—clear, sharp-scented—into her palm and flicked the drops in a neat cross into the water. The smell was Florida water cologne: citrus, spice, a barber's clean memory. She did it as one does sweeping—practical, without theatre.

The man at the pole looked to the woman for his cue and got it. He set the pirogue's flat nose against the root with a bump that sounded like a kiss and held her there with the pole as if pinning a goat for shoeing. The woman's feet found the crossbench. She stepped to the root with a balance that made the water forget it had arguments. She stood above Artemis a moment, not disdaining to look long.

Close, her face showed more history than age, a handsome severity softened at the corners by use and mercy. A silver holy medal lay at her throat; the saint had been rubbed thin until the face was a smooth wish. Her hands were clean and smelled of camphor. When she bent, the indigo sleeve rode back and showed a bracelet of cowrie shells that made a dry whisper when she moved. She put her fingers to Artemis's wrist where the blood stammers when afraid and listened with her thumb. She nodded to herself as at a market stall: not bad, not good. Enough.

"Drink slow," she said, and put to Artemis's lips a spoon with the smallest dampness in it—water sweetened with something dark and slow, cane syrup perhaps, or blackstrap thinned and made kind. Artemis tasted it like confession. The spoon came again and again in measures that felt like law. The woman waited between each offering as if witnessing a vow. There was no pity in

her, only a careful stewardship that took its work seriously.

"You have a name?" the woman asked when the spoon had done what spoons can. Her French smelled like home to itself—Louisiana, not France—and her English stepped with a Creole's gait. She did not hurry.

Artemis moved her lips and the sound came like a boot across gravel. "Ar—temis."

The woman nodded. "Artémise," she repeated in her mouth, changing the weight of the syllables, making it belong to this place without asking permission. She touched Artemis's cheek with three fingers, very lightly. "Bon. I am Éloise," she said. "Mère Éloise to some; Éloise to God when I scold Him. You fell out the sea into my pocket, so I'll take you up, mais? Baptiste, doucement. Lift."

The man at the pole—Baptiste—stepped onto the root with a carefulness that had been taught by many broken ankles. He was river-brown and long-backed, a scar making a small story near his ear. He did not look at Artemis the way men look when they mean to take. He looked the way men look when they mean to carry a sack of rice through mud and not lose a grain. Together they slid arms beneath hatch and woman and canvas and made a parcel of the whole, letting the water bear its share without protest. The barrel they left; the barrel did not belong to any life that had more minutes in it.

Artemis bared her teeth at the first motion because pain thinks it is a person and must be introduced. The world swayed. She shut one eye to keep it from spilling. Mère Éloise murmured—not to her; perhaps to the root,

perhaps to the day: a run of words with Latin in their bones and something older beside it, a psalm worn to the soft by use.

They slid her into the pirogue and the boat sighed around her weight. The boards were warm where the woman had sat; the smell of them was sap and work. Baptiste pushed off with a small grunt. The pirogue moved as if it had been waiting all morning for the pleasure. Water sewed itself shut behind them with neat little noises. Once Baptiste dipped the pole and it came up with a garter of weed and a small turtle clinging, indignant; he flicked it away as if rejecting a joke.

Artemis lay with the canvas over her cheek, sky rim bright beyond, and watched the world pass in new grammar. The trees walked. The water made the same small case again and again for being taken seriously. A blue bottle tree appeared on a hump of ground—dead limbs set with glass to catch wickedness the way a salt box catches weevils—and the sight of it soothed her without explaining itself. An altar under a cypress wore offerings: a cup of coffee filmed over; three pennies; a cigar stub; two white candles guttering like tired lungs. Mère Éloise crossed herself in the old habit and lifted a shoulder at the same time as if reminding the saints that she would do the work whether they came or not.

"Wreckers been at it down by the bar," Baptiste said in a voice made to be had not heard. "Storm spit plenty, Mère."

"Et alors?" Mère Éloise did not look at him.

"Plenty eyes hungry. Men see a thing the sea gives and call it theirs."

The woman's gaze slid to Artemis like a hand that knows its owner. "Sea gives. Land keeps," she said, and the phrase had the weight of a proverb. She did not explain which thing the land meant to keep.

They came round a bend and a house revealed itself the way a creature reveals its young: by degrees and with pride. It stood up out of water on cypress posts with a skirt of shadow beneath. The planks had been hand-planed into obedience. A gallery ran along the front, its rail hung with drying things: fish like punctuation marks; bundles of leaves; a snakeskin turned inside out and pegged up like a long glove. Bottles of different blues hung from a crepe myrtle and chimed the smallest glass bells when a wind remembered to come through. Chickens stepped about on palmetto fans laid for tidiness. A shrine at one corner held saints who had learned to live peaceably with others: St. Michael in tin; Our Lady in a blue that remembered oceans; a little rough-carved statue wearing red beads that might, in another mouth, have been called a warrior. Between them a saucer of cane syrup shone dark; a cup of water waited immaculate.

Baptiste bumped the pirogue against a runged ladder and caught the rung with his toe as if the house and his body had been rehearsing this for years. Two girls came to the top of the steps—one tall and braid-sober, the other younger and feral at the eyes—and peered down as if a fish had asked for admittance. Mère Éloise did not turn.

"Cloth," she said. "The white one. And heat on. Camphor. And bring the little bottle with the woman on it." The girls scattered, feet like small weather.

"Doucement, Baptiste," she said, and he nodded though no roughness had entered him.

The steps were a trial and Artemis made of herself something that could be trialled. Boards met her back that had the memory of sun in them. The house's air pressed, but with purpose; she understood that she was inside a body that knew its work.

The room they took her to was narrow and thoughtful. Mosquito netting made milky walls. A table bore tools that were not tools: mortar and pestle scrubbed clean, bundles tied in red thread, a jar of clear with things sleeping in it that might have once been snakes. A square of mirror had been leaned against the wall and a prayer card tucked into its frame like a debt paid. There was a bed, iron, with a rosary looped twice around one post as if to make the metal remember mercy. Mère Éloise's hand went to that rosary and flicked it once, not to ask but to announce.

"Water," she said, and the tall girl appeared with a blue-and-white bowl, its rim chipped into a familiar history. Mère Éloise dipped a rag, wrung, laid it across Artemis's forehead as if smoothing a page. The cloth smelled of something clean and sweet and faintly floral—the bottle with the woman on it, perhaps, that had been in the basket: Florida Water turned liturgy. Then camphor came—she broke it under her fingers and the room remembered winter, remembered breath without struggle.

"Not too much," she told the girl, and the girl listened with her whole mouth. "We bring her back by the corners. Not all at once. People break when you pull too quick."

She worked down Artemis's arms with the cloth, untying sludge and salt and the unkind hands of the night. She unfastened the bodice with the impersonal decency of a midwife and turned Artemis enough to learn where the skin had been scoured and where it would soon complain. She said *tsk* once, as if scolding the sea not for cruelty but for slovenliness. She flicked her fingers and the younger girl ran with a little pot of fat. The fat smelled of bear and herbs and a promise. Mère Éloise warmed some on her palm and pressed it gently into torn places until the skin learned to believe it was still part of the body.

"Who you lost," Mère Éloise said. Not a question, only a door left open.

Artemis found the shape of the boy's hand in her sleeve and could not find his name without blood. "A child," she said, voice made of wire. "A boy. Michael." She swallowed and the swallow clicked. "And more."

"We set a light for them," Mère Éloise said, as you say: we set out bread. "This house keeps a table. The dead, they got manners, too." She looked at the tall girl. "Two candles. Not red."

The girl went. The smaller girl hovered, fiercer than any cat, then, as if affronted by a kindness she did not yet know how to repay, fled.

Baptiste stood at the doorpost and made himself part of wood. He watched only the space beyond the net, as a man does when his job is to be wall and witness both. Once he looked at Artemis, properly, and his mouth did a small thing that was not smile and not pity. He had a scar; scars recognize one another.

"Eat?" he asked, hesitant, as if offering a word he did not trust.

"Non," Mère Éloise answered. "Later."

She brought a porcelain spoon of something that was more than water and less than food. "Sip. Keep it." She rationed the sips the way a good woman rations sugar before the boat from town.

Heat rose and the house breathed with her. At the room's far corner on a small table under a cloth a space had been made for petition: a bottle of rum sealed tight; a dish of eggs; a length of red thread; a saucer of salt that had not yet learned this air. Mère Éloise set two candles there and struck a match. The fire caught obediently and made of itself not drama but work. She said no words that would let a stranger name them. She only stood and looked, and the looking had thanks in it and a little bargaining and something like apology.

Artemis drifted. Sleep came in sheets pulled up and then down by a mother busy with other tasks. The house went on being house: footsteps; a kettle protesting; a child outside trying on a laugh too big and discovering it did not yet fit; the pleased mutter of chickens; a bottle clinking a blue bell against its neighbour when wind remembered to come through. She woke to find the holy medal's face smooth as ever against Mère Éloise's skin. The woman had fallen asleep sitting, jaw set, hand still on Artemis's arm as if to remind the body that the world had decided to keep it.

Night again, because time in this place was not hours but humours. Candlelight made saints honest. Baptiste murmured to someone on the gallery and the someone's

voice answered in a high eager run. "Pas de bruit," he said, and the child smothered the rest of the sentence under both hands like a secret. Mère Éloise woke without startling and went to the corner table, moved a thing, added a coin to the saucer, lifted the rum's cork and let its smell breathe, then stoppered it again. She crossed herself with the impatience of a woman marking her place in a book when the pot boils over.

When she came back Artemis was awake enough to arrange words. "Why—" she began, and had to find another word because *why* is a wide net and catches too much. "Who are you to me?"

Mère Éloise considered the ceiling as if it held the answer written in damp and ghost of smoke. "I am the one the water put you to," she said. "That's enough for today." She slid her palm under Artemis's hand and held it, not soft. "The sea gives. The land keeps. We will see what the land wants."

"You keep me?" Artemis meant to say *save*, meant to say *help*, but her mouth, honest from salt, chose the other.

"Keep can be many ways," Mère Éloise said, and neither the candle nor the mirror corrected her.

Artemis closed her eyes because sleep wanted to try again. In the dark behind lids she saw the aunt's hand lifted like a small formal blessing; the Cornishman's arm hooking her belt; the cardman's face, open to weather, with the oilskin at his throat; Michael's brow, set with determination stolen from a man. She reached for the fragments and they arranged themselves briefly into a

floor she could stand upon. When they fell apart again, she did not fall with them.

The house settled the way living things do when they intend to go on. Mère Éloise tied a small bag of something to the headboard—seeds perhaps, or hair, or iron filings. She spat in it, cinched the string, and knocked it twice so it would listen. "Pas méchant," she told it, and the bag agreed to behave. She drew the net properly around bed and woman and fixed its hem under the mattress like tucking a child.

At the threshold she paused and spoke into the house without turning her head. "You heard me," she said. "Nou gen moun la a*." We have a person here. The sentence included the saints, the river, the women whose pictures leaned in frames, the bottles, the snakeskin, and the things unnamed that minded corners. "Behave." The house, in the way of houses, promised nothing and complied.

Artemis slept this time like someone who has paid for it. The swamp's choir kept liturgy. In the middle of the night a wind crossed the gallery and shook the blue bottles into speech. Mère Éloise rose, went out, and answered them in that language that is made of hand and salt and thread. Dawn scratched at the eaves with the carelessness of a chicken. Baptiste, who did not sleep like ordinary men, was already on the steps, his feet remembering river before his head remembered names.

Artemis woke with the memory of hands pressing dough into obedience and understood it had been her own skin. She turned her head and found that turning had become something a body might do for pleasure one day, if it set out early and did not hurry. Mère Éloise

stood at the little shrine with the two candles guttering dutifully toward their ends. She set a third, small, and let it take. "Pour les noyés," she said, and did not look to see whether Artemis understood. For the drowned.

"Merci," Artemis said, and did not know to whom the thanks rightly belonged.

Mère Éloise turned then, smiling with one corner of her mouth as if that was all she could spare at this hour. "Eat now," she said. "Just broth." She lifted the spoon and Artemis, obedient as an infant and feeling the clean humiliation of it, opened her mouth.

Behind the woman's shoulder the mirror on the table caught the room askew: Artemis's face, altered by salt; the candle's patient labour; the shapes on the shrine that did not quarrel with one another. In the mirror there was also the window and, in the window, the world beyond: a cypress with grey beard; a white bird stepping sideways like a learned man; a thin line of smoke that did not belong to this house.

Others had seen the storm's harvest. Others would come.

Mère Éloise followed Artemis's glance and nodded as if a page had turned at last. "The sea sends," she said. "The hungry follow. Eat, Artémise. Tomorrow, we bind what is loose. And you will speak all your names."

Names. She had only one she trusted. It felt different here, heavier, as if the air had put coins in its hem.

"Artemis Danger," she said, and the room learned her.

"Bon," Mère Éloise said. "Danger." She let the word sit on her tongue and smiled fully now, not with happiness but with understanding. "The land keeps what suits it."

She set a hand on the net and knotted its corner with a gesture that was more than tidiness and less than spell. "Sleep again," she instructed. "I will sit."

Artemis allowed herself the softness of obedience. The candle burned small as a fingernail's moon. The house carried her counting for her. Outside, the veils swayed and told one another the news: what the storm had done; what the river intended; that a woman had been fished from salt and given over to trees.

"The sea gives; the land keeps."

Chapter VII – The Priestess

"Rescue and capture are sometimes the same hand."
— Proverb overheard in Congo Square, 1851

The bed learned her shape. For two days Artemis moved only between sleep and broth, her body deciding for her. The broth was of bones and bitter herbs; the taste clung to the back of her tongue like counsel. Each spoonful brought back another inch of the world until she could stand it again.

The house went on around her, its life as steady as a pump's rhythm. Girls quarrelled and reconciled, clattering their wooden shoes across the gallery. Baptiste's voice came low and even, conversing with animals, with weather, with wood as he planed it. Mère Éloise moved with the calm of a woman who had not asked for company but would do the job properly now that it was in her care.

Artemis's body mended in small accounts: the swelling in her hands abated; the raw rope burns closed like stitched mouths; her lips lost their cracks and became lips again. But healing, she realized, was not free. For each measure given, something was quietly asked.

On the third night she woke to the smell of smoke that was not firewood. Candles burned on the little table, their light hunched low. Mère Éloise sat with her hands busy, weaving thread through a circle of leaves and bones no bigger than a handspan. She did not look up, though Artemis's eyes opened.

"You stir," she said. Her voice was even, not surprised. "Good. The broth found its work."

"What... is that?" Artemis asked, her mouth dry from silence.

"A guard," Mère Éloise said simply. "For the bed. For you."

The shape in her lap was both crude and precise: feathers braided through string, a wishbone fixed at the centre, a charm bag tied in red. Artemis felt her throat tighten. It was not Catholic, not the prayers she had been raised on. But there was discipline in it, something ancient and exact.

Mère Éloise's eyes lifted and found her, wet bark glinting in the candle. "You fear it?"

"I don't know it."

"Not knowing is often the same thing." She set the circle down on the floor beside the bed, muttered in a tongue that was French and something older, then pressed her thumb into the dirt-stained boards as if signing a contract. "Sleep," she said, not request but order.

And Artemis, despite herself, obeyed.

By day she walked the gallery, her legs trembling with the newness of standing. Beyond the rail stretched swamp: water black and brown, veils of moss shifting like gowns, insects stitching the air with silver threads of sound. The house was not island but root among roots. No path met it. Only boats came, and only those who knew the water's grammar could manage them.

The younger girl—Léonie—followed Artemis with a mistrustful hunger, as cats follow the smell of milk. The elder—Celeste—helped her down the steps and taught her

to rinse herself at a basin where rainwater pooled. Celeste's hands were quick and dutiful, never soft. Léonie's eyes, though, were knives: amused, suspicious, sharp as if already carving her into the story she would tell later.

One afternoon Baptiste set a stool near the water and showed her how to clean fish with a blade no longer than a finger. He worked in silence, sliding knife through belly, rinsing blood away with the same economy as if he were splitting wood. Artemis mirrored the motions, clumsy, then steadier. The fish's silver sides glared like accusation. She found she could not meet their eyes.

"You cut," Baptiste said finally, voice as measured as his strokes. "You eat. That's all. Don't dress it prettier."

It was the longest sentence she had heard him give. She nodded.

Night was different. Candles burned in the corner shrine; rum was poured; beads glimmered like low stars. Mère Éloise's voice wove through the rooms in songs that were not lullabies but something sterner, binding. Sometimes she touched Artemis's arm when she passed, as if checking a pulse without needing fingers. Once she placed a pouch—stitched in red, filled with seeds and iron filings—under her pillow.

"You keep this," she said. "For sleep. For spirit."

Artemis held it in her palm, light as a bird. "Why me?" she asked, before she could stop herself.

Mère Éloise smiled with half her mouth. "Because the sea spat you on my step. That makes you mine until I say otherwise."

The words landed heavy, not cruel, not kind. Ownership spoken as casually as weather. Artemis set the pouch under the pillow and lay awake long after, staring at the net that trembled with every breath.

On the fifth day she tried the ladder, meaning to put her foot to the swamp and feel the ground of the new world beneath her. Celeste stopped her with a hand hard as oak.

"Not for you," she said.

"Why?"

The girl shrugged. "Maman says."

"Mère Éloise?"

"She knows what walks," Celeste answered, and did not explain.

Artemis looked out across the still black water, the veils swaying like slow dancers. Something stirred there, heavy and unseen. She remembered the blunt back of the manatee, the slow menace of the fin. She stepped back up without arguing.

That night Mère Éloise came to her with a bowl that steamed sharp and green. "Drink."

Artemis obeyed. The taste was bitter, teeth-coating, but the warmth spread down her body like a hand smoothing sheet. Her vision blurred, then cleared into strangeness. The rafters above seemed longer than they had been. The netting quivered as if something leaned against it from the outside. She saw, in the bowl's dark, the curve of a boy's cheek—Michael's—and a hand lifting in farewell.

She set the bowl down with shaking hands. "What is this?"

"Medicine," Mère Éloise said. Her voice was kind, but in the corner of her mouth lay a secret that was not. "For the body. For the spirit. For binding what is loose."

Artemis lay back. The candlelight bent and folded into shadows that had weight. Somewhere beyond the gallery, a drumbeat carried faint, as if someone were striking the swamp's ribs with their palm. She felt her limbs turn heavy, her thoughts scatter. Before sleep took her she realized something simple and terrifying:

Rescue and capture are sometimes the same hand.

''A gift may be a tether''

Chapter VIII – Hunger & Omen

"Before a door is shut, the threshold is taught its work."
— Saying among root workers, collected 1840s

Hunger returned first, like a stray that remembered the road to her ribcage. Not the clean want of bread after work, but a different creature—trained, watchful. Mère Éloise fed her as one measures medicine: spoon, pause, breath; spoon, pause, breath. "Too much will harm," she said, and Artemis believed her at first because it mattered how belief was spent. Broth thickened to porridge, porridge to fish, but never enough to make a body foolish with ease.

"Fasting clears the glass," Celeste offered in her careful English, lowering her eyes as if the sentence had been borrowed and must be returned unchipped. "For dreams."

"Dreams of what?" Artemis asked.

"Of who," Léonie said, and smiled with her teeth.

The house kept rules without announcing them. Brooms leaned with their bristles up. A penny glinted under the threshold—caught sunlight like an eye. The doorframes bore neat crosses of something citrus-bitter that stung her nose; the same smell Mère Éloise had flicked on the water. Bottles sang when wind passed. Pins sat in a saucer with their heads all facing east, obedient and peculiar. None of it threatened; all of it worked.

Artemis's hands forgot salt and learned camphor, learned fat rubbed into skin until skin forgave. She mended her shift with a needle Celeste gave her and afterward could not find the thread-ends she had cut.

Someone had tidied too carefully. Someone collected ends.

On the second morning she woke to find a small braid coiled on the table like something shed by a snake. Her hand flew to her head and found the parting neat, a lock taken with a dressmaker's care.

"You were hot," Celeste said, unembarrassed, holding up the scissors. "We cooled you. Keeps fever from rooting."

Hair is a confession and a signature both. Artemis smiled and thanked her, because the world had made a habit of taking and she had learned the grammar of surviving: you do not scold the tide. But later, when the girls went to the gallery to quarrel softly over who would pluck a chicken, she stood before the mirror shard and traced the new absence with two fingers. She thought of seeds and pockets and the small bags tied in red, and the place at the back of her neck went cold.

Baptiste taught her to move with the house, not against it. "Step after step," he said, showing her the ladder—how to put one foot where water will lay it down softly. "You lean into air like this," and his body did what bodies do when they belong to water. He kept his gaze off her face, careful as a man walking with a full pail.

"Why not the boat?" Artemis asked, cheerful in tone, casual as hunger lets. The pirogue sat with its nose raised, flirtatious with mud, pole propped like a rifle.

He touched the hull with his knuckles, then the topmost rung of the ladder. "This one," he said, indicating the ladder, "never runs away." The boat he left unpraised.

She tried the rung with her toe and found a smear of pale stuff across it, hard to see unless one's eyes were taught. Salt? No—this was softer, a paste that wore herbs. It smelled like someone else's prayer. She drew back as if the rung had teeth. Baptiste's mouth did the small not-smile again. He did not speak. He had already explained.

That night Mère Éloise gave her a bowl whose steam smelled green and strict. "Sip," she said. "For closing the gates that want to stay open too late." The taste was bitter and clean both, like truth. It swam behind the eyes. After, Artemis lay on her side under netting that made milk of the air, and the room made new angles. Shadows took up their instruments and tuned.

Dreams came in serviceable images: a card deck bound in oilskin, a wishbone tied with red thread, a hatch turning forever in a brown river like the idea of a door with no house to fit. Michael stood beside the bed with his cap in his hand and corrected her counting with the seriousness of a magistrate. When she reached to touch his sleeve, her fingers came back smelling of Florida water, and the dream shrugged and became something else: a white bird stepping sideways on a cypress knee; the bird tilted its head and said her name in a man's voice she did not know.

She woke without startle and found the bowl still under her breath, the net still drawn, and Mère Éloise seated in her chair with her arms folded, asleep like soldiering. On the little table the two candles for the drowned had worn their way down and been replaced without theatre. The house had its liturgy. She belonged to the congregation only as someone's guest—until a guest learns the work.

In the morning Artemis opened the cardman's oilskin at last. The thong had shrunk to cruelty; she worried it open with her teeth and the small sailor's knife and apologized in her head to the dead as if he owned the knot still. Inside, the pasteboards had glued themselves into a fan with salt. She teased them one by one until the paper forgave, careful as a woman unpicking someone else's hem. Most bore no picture—only pips—slicked toward anonymity, stained with men's thumbs. Two still held faces not yet drowned: a queen with a cup, a tower struck.

"Bon," Léonie said from the doorway, a girl who knew how to enter without a sound. "You like cards."

"I like company," Artemis said, laying the Queen face-up on the windowsill as if giving her air.

"Careful." Léonie reached, then drew back hands that were small and sure. "Things breathe when you set them like that."

"What things?"

"The ones that want to ride," Léonie replied, with the assurance of a child who has never been disbelieved by the house. She sniffed the room, wrinkled her nose. "Maman says go slow with you. You got storms still in you. They don't like to share."

Artemis slid the Queen back under oilskin with the feeling of covering a mirror after a wake. Hunger pinched. She wrapped it in the more polite words. "Is there bread?"

"Later," Léonie sang, already halfway gone, "if you behave."

Behave means stay.

By noon two pirogues passed the house single-file—the men in them not looking at the gallery, which is a way of looking. Salvage lay heaped in the forward boats like offerings: staves, coils of line, a barrel head, a chest whose lock had failed. One man had an anchor on his shoulder and the pride of it made his eyes golden. Baptiste watched without greeting. Mère Éloise came to the rail and lowered her chin in a gesture that turned into nothing, not acknowledgement, not refusal.

"Wreckers," Artemis said, the Dublin quay in her mouth remembering a different word—pilferers, gleaners, saints of the littoral depending who tells it.

"Hmm," Mère Éloise said, the syllable a drawer that closed without showing you what had been put inside. "The sea gives. Land keeps. Some men keep more than others."

A length of rope dropped from the pirogue and fetched water with a slap. The man at the stern fished it up with a hook, scolded it, and did not look up again. Artemis watched the rope trail a thin line of red—not blood, but paint—breadcrumbs for anyone who needed to know which path the boats had laid across the swamp. She logged it in the small ledger her mind now kept: routes, noises, habits, the hour at which Celeste's hands were busiest, the hour Mère Éloise sat to plait and knot.

That evening Celeste combed Artemis's hair as if fishing in a shallow stream. Comb, water, oil, comb. Halfway through she paused and drew out something caught near the scalp: a tiny packet tied in thread, as if the house itself had made a burr and carried it to her. Celeste's

mouth tightened. She slid the thing into her skirt pocket with an adult's haste. Later Artemis fished for it in the washing basket and found it tucked deeper than the pocket went: a cloth the size of a thumb, damp with something sweet, threaded with three of her hairs and a sliver of nail.

"You drop this," she said to no one, and laid it upon the shrine table beside the saucer of water as if returning a book late but honest. In the mirror's skewed glass she saw Mère Éloise behind her, expression arranged into that soft corner-smile that meant yes and no in one motion.

"Allez," the woman said mildly. "I keep what I keep. You keep what you keep." She plucked the packet from the table and put it somewhere the mirror was not invited.

"Why me?" Artemis asked. She did not put all the words on the question.

Mère Éloise did not pretend confusion. "Because your door is open," she said. "You were in the sea; all your names got washed thin. A spirit sees a woman like that and wants to try her on. We feed you little so you hear better. We wash you so they smell you clean. We keep you so you don't go running to somebody who keeps worse."

It was honest and it was not. Artemis turned the sentence until it showed its other face. "And then?" she asked.

Mère Éloise shrugged, a motion with the weight of a law. "We see."

Sleep that night had corners. She turned them and found small things placed there: a dish of salt under the bed—stubborn crystals refusing to melt in this air; a sprig of something bitter looped over the curtain rod; chalk lines faint as breath on the floor between bed and door, the exact geometry of restraint.

"Rescue and capture," Artemis said into the netting, and the net held the words as if they were a moth that must be let go later.

Her hunger took on voice by morning. The little porridge bowl came late and did not satisfy. When she washed the spoon clean, she put it under the pallet, an instinct older than shame. When Celeste came with a second spoon, she set it in plain sight and smiled, a woman who had never stolen anything except an hour's peace.

"Walk," Baptiste suggested, tilting his head toward the gallery. He walked with her, slow as someone in a sickroom, along the long boards to the corner where bottles of different blues hung like a cages for weather. "Here the wind," he said. It came; it did not. He put his palm above the rail and she copied the gesture and felt something move across it, not air exactly, but a pressure with memory attached.

"You don't go," he said. "Not now."

"Not ever?" She let the question ask only half.

He eased his shoulders. "You hear? Drums at night? Out by St. John." He meant Bayou St. John, the thread that stitched lake to city. "People ride. They get lost if

the house don't hold them. Mère Éloise hold them, sometimes."

"By keeping me?" Artemis asked. He did not answer because men working for capable women learn to let certain questions pass like fish through fingers. He pointed to the sky. A vulture made a neat circle and then another, auditioner in black. "He not for you," he said. "Not yet."

"Comforting," she said dryly, and his mouth did the small not-smile that was not contempt.

Toward evening, omens crowded like guests that drink their host's wine. A snake skin shed under the steps left like a glove; Léonie found it, squealed, then pegged it to the rail with pride for evil eyes to tangle in. A jar in the corner bubbled once, though no one touched it. The penny under the threshold winked and was gone; when Artemis bent to look, there were three pennies and a nail standing upright in the seam of the floor, held by nothing seeable. Mère Éloise's hands were busy with a figure of cloth the size of Artemis's palm—plain muslin, no face, a fishbone stitched where a spine should be. "For health," she said without being asked, and jabbed the needle into the cloth's shoulder with more tenderness than seemed possible and more dignity than any doll had a right to own.

It would be a poppet in other mouths; here, it was a point of attention.

"May I?" Artemis asked, surprising herself.

Mère Éloise passed her the needle as if passing a cup. Artemis stitched her own hair into the seam at the hem,

two strands only, and tied the knot with a washerwoman's stubbornness. "So I know where I am," she said, and that truth did not bruise anyone. Mère Éloise watched, pleased.

"You clever," the woman said. "I like clever. Foolish people break or burn." She tapped the muslin shoulder with one finger, a blessing or a warning. "You will sit for me tomorrow. Just to listen. Not long."

"To what?"

"The ones who want to borrow you," Mère Éloise said. "We see who has manners."

Artemis smiled with her mouth and withhold her teeth. "And if they don't?"

"We don't answer the door." Mère Éloise's glance said: I have shut many doors. She stroked the poppet's seam smooth. "Hunger teaches your ribs to make a bell," she added. "Spirits like bells; they ring easy."

Artemis went to bed early because there is dignity in choosing your own departure. She put the sailor's knife under the mattress where muslin wore thin. She placed the cardman's oilskin beneath the pallet board where a mouse had chewed a crescent. She retied the pouch under her pillow tighter than before and spat once, polite but firm, the way she had seen Mère Éloise speak to the invisible. Then she counted: board knots across the ceiling; breaths; the seconds between bottle chimes. When sleep came it came on small feet like a child allowed back into a room after sulking.

Night offered her the usual, and something else. She woke at the hour when rooms confess their cracks and

saw the chalk lines at the threshold in brighter thread, as if someone had drawn with light under the first drawing. The net stirred in no wind. A low sound moved the air: not drum, not hymn, the hush of men poling in a line. She went to the window and lifted the edge of the cloth and found the world outside arranged for lesson. Three pirogues slid by, polite as undertakers. The men in them had tied white cloths around their arms for notice—not mourning, not surrender, a truce with the dark. One boat carried a drafted thing: a cross made of wood dragged from the lake, knotted with riverweed, candles stuck and burning along its length so the wax fell like small prayers.

Baptiste sat on the steps, bareheaded, and made no sign to them; he belonged to the water and the water was busy. Mère Éloise stood shadowed at the door and did not cross the threshold. Her hands were empty, which was a kind of weapon.

Artemis let the cloth fall. She lay back down and rehearsed the posture of docility until her shoulders learned it. "Tomorrow," she told the knife, which is a way of telling oneself: be a hinge; be a door, not a wall.

At daybreak the house tasted of coffee and camphor. Celeste set a white skirt for her, laundered until it had its own light. Léonie combed the little braids flat and patted the part where hair had lately been. Mère Éloise drew a line of chalk on the floor between bed and table and another circle within which the chair had been placed.

"Sit," she said. "No more than a bowl's worth of time."

"What bowl?"

"The blue one." She smiled. "You will know when it empties."

Artemis stepped into the circle and the air changed temperature by a degree, no more than the difference between shade and sun, but it had an intention to it. She sat. Her hunger struck the bell that lived where ribs are. The bottles pinged once in agreement.

Mère Éloise made a sign in the air that was not Europe's cross and was not not it. She set down rum and coffee and a plate with three slices of bread: one for the dead, one for the living, one untouched. She whispered names and withheld names with equal courtesy. Baptiste leaned in the doorway, long as a mast. Celeste and Léonie stood at the edge of the room with palms hidden in skirts to keep from reaching where they should not.

"Listen," Mère Éloise told Artemis, and laid a hand on the crown of her head, not heavy.

Artemis closed her eyes. The world sorted itself. Threshold. Chalk. A small pop as a candle accepted being fire. The first breath that was not hers standing beside hers and finding the measure. She counted, because numbers made a path back.

Then, like a fish surfacing where you thought the river exhausted, a name in a voice she knew nothing about: something that smelled of salt and iron and old wood. Not Michael. Not the cardman. Something with patience and the weight of places. It did not knock. It asked, the way a tide asks: again, and again.

Artemis did what clever women do. She stepped back inside herself one pace and smiled without showing

teeth. "No," she said, in the tone of a woman refusing a second slice of cake, and kept the word behind her teeth like a pin.

Mère Éloise's fingers approved. "Bon," she murmured.

The blue bowl turned its own emptiness without help. Somewhere outside a bird stropped its bill against a branch. The smell of coffee changed meanings: first welcome, then warning. The circle's chalk warmed under her soles.

"Enough," Mère Éloise said at last. She lifted her hand. The room corrected itself, slowly. Bread sat where bread had been. The untouched slice remained a promise on a plate. Artemis's hunger rang once, twice, then settled to a hum she could talk over.

"Tomorrow," Mère Éloise said, casual as weather. "We draw the big circle."

Artemis nodded as if the day had placed a minor task on her lap. "I'll wear the white," she said, and her voice did not betray the knife beneath the mattress, the spoon under the pallet, the inventory of routes in her head like beads on a string.

Rescue and capture are sometimes the same hand. So is escape and invitation.

She smiled back with only the rightful portion of gratitude and went to wash her hands as if preparing to knead dough. In the mirror shard the room tilted into its other self: bottle bells; chalk; the small poppet with a fishbone spine. She touched the white skirt and thought of salt-streaked sails. The house watched, approving and untroubled.

Before a door is shut, the threshold is taught its work.

She would learn the bridgework of thresholds tonight—
the loose plank, the soft rung, the inch of floor that
complained—so that when the circle opened tomorrow, a
different door would open for her as well.

Chapter VIX – The Circle Drawn

"A circle is a mouth that may swallow,
or a wall that may save.
Only the hand that draws it knows which."
— Attributed to a Louisiana conjure-woman, 1852

The floor had been swept until it showed its grain like muscle under skin. Chalk lines lay across it in neat geometry: cross, arc, circle within circle. The white skirt Celeste had pressed for her smelled of starch and camphor; when Artemis lowered herself into it, the fabric whispered against her bones. She was set in the centre chair like a token in a game whose rules she was only learning.

Candles ringed the room, their flames taut and thin. A bottle of rum stood open, its neck exhaling a sharp sweetness. Coffee steamed in a blue bowl, thick and bitter. Bread, cut in three slices, waited on a plate at the shrine. Salt in a shallow dish reflected the light like a second set of eyes.

Mère Éloise moved barefoot, her indigo skirts brushing the chalk but never smudging it. She sprinkled a powder—ash, crushed shell, perhaps bone dust—in a slow circle around Artemis's chair. Baptiste leaned against the doorframe, arms folded, his presence part watchman, part anchor. Celeste and Léonie hovered at the edge, restless, fascinated, nervous in the way of children told to stand still at a funeral.

"You sit quiet," Mère Éloise instructed, voice low and calm. "You listen. You don't answer unless I tell you. If something knocks, you don't open. If it calls your name, you don't turn your head. Understand?"

Artemis nodded. Her throat was dry, but her silence was solid.

"Good." Mère Éloise tapped her breastbone twice with a finger dampened in rum, then tapped Artemis the same way, as though tying two knots with one string.

The ritual began with sound. Éloise sang in a voice like water running through wood, syllables that were not French, not Latin, but carried both in their bones. Her hands moved slow as the song's pulse, lifting bread, pouring coffee, setting them down in deliberate measure. The house seemed to join her; bottles on the porch chimed, a board creaked and then held its tongue, the swamp itself leaned closer with insect-hum and frog-throat.

Artemis felt her hunger at once: sharp, ringing, a bell struck under her ribs. The bitter tea she'd drunk earlier left her mouth dry, her body hollowed. She realized Éloise had planned it so—the body made lean, spirit easier to sound like a drumskin.

At first there was nothing but the woman's voice and the scrape of her own pulse. Then—softly, slyly—an answering murmur pressed against the air. Not words. More like pressure, like a second room crowding into the first. The candles bent as if all the wicks leaned toward one breath.

Something moved close to Artemis's ear. She felt it more than heard it—a whisper-shaped absence, syllables without vowels. Michael's name rose in her throat like a sob, but she bit it hard before it left her mouth. She remembered Éloise's instruction: don't answer. Don't turn.

Another voice pushed against her skin, this one almost tender. Her mother's. *Artemis, a stór, come out now, come out of the cold.* The inflection was exact. She clenched her fists in her lap until her nails scored her palm. She had seen her mother buried; she knew the voice was not hers.

Her silence tasted like blood.

Éloise's singing rose, sharp as command. She flung a handful of powder into the air—scented, pungent, something that stung the nose and made the eyes water. The pressure around Artemis recoiled. The air cleared, though the hunger under her ribs thrummed louder, as though pleased with itself.

"Bon," Mère Éloise said between verses. "You listen well."

Not all the voices retreated. One lingered, patient, heavy as iron. It pressed the air with the weight of tides. Artemis did not know its name, but it knew hers. She felt it at the base of her skull, a whisper without sound, a presence that wanted to set anchor inside her chest.

Her body betrayed her. She swayed forward, lips parting.

"Non," Mère Éloise snapped, voice sharp as a lash. Her hand shot out and clamped Artemis's chin, forcing her mouth shut. The old woman's bark of laughter was not cruel but triumphant, as if pleased the test had come. "This one tries. She strong. But we stronger."

Éloise lifted her face toward the rafters and barked a string of words like hammer-blows. The thing withdrew—not defeated, only delayed. Artemis felt it loosen, leave,

as a claw loosens from cloth. The absence left a bruise behind her eyes.

The candles righted themselves. The air smelled of ash and bitter root. Mère Éloise set the bread slice on the plate for the dead and nodded once, satisfied. "Enough." She rubbed her hands clean as if shedding dust, then looked at Artemis.

"You carry storm still," she said. "They smell it on you. They want to live inside it. You shut your door good tonight."

Artemis drew breath through her teeth, slow, careful. Her whole body shook with fatigue. "And if I hadn't?"

Éloise's smile was small, dangerous. "Then you belong to what knocks."

That night she could not sleep. The chalk had been wiped away, the candles snuffed, but she still felt the circle drawn around her skin, as though Éloise's powder had marked her deeper than flesh. The hunger in her belly grew sharper for being denied. She drank from the rain-basin until her stomach ached, but water was not what her body wanted.

From the porch she heard Baptiste humming, slow, tuneless, a sound to anchor boats. From the kitchen Celeste and Léonie whispered and giggled, their voices slipping through the cracks. She thought of the knives hung on the wall, the little bags stitched with hair and nail, the braid taken from her head. She thought of the word *keep*.

Tomorrow, Éloise had said. Tomorrow, the big circle.

Artemis turned her face into the pillow and let her mind walk instead. She mapped the steps between bed and door, door and ladder, ladder to the pirogue. She counted the boards that groaned underfoot. She measured the house as if it were already behind her.

Sleep came at last. But in her dream the chalk lines had followed her, winding through the swamp, white against black water, a net with no end. And far off, a boy's voice kept counting—seventy-two, fifty-six, seventy-two—angry at himself for losing the thread.

The First Circle Binds, The Second Decides"

Chapter X – Silence As Weapon

"Close your mouth and keep your map."
— Saying among women who survive

Silence had been her companion on the ship—born of shyness, sharpened by hunger. In the swamp it became an instrument. On the morning after the circle, Artemis woke with the taste of chalk in her teeth and decided to put down speech like a tool she would not lend.

She tested it at breakfast. Celeste brought a tin bowl, porridge thin and proper. Artemis raised the spoon, ate, nodded thanks, and did not spend a single word. Celeste waited for a question and, when none came, frowned as if the grammar of the room had slipped.

"Pain?" she asked in her soft English.

Artemis shook her head.

"You angry?" Léonie demanded, sharp as a fishbone.

Artemis smiled, a small candle, then let it gutter.

Mère Éloise watched from the doorway with her arms folded, mouth set at its usual patient corner. "Bon," she said. "A day of closed tongue makes a tight vessel. But know what you do." She lifted a hand, palm outward, without the bother of blessing. "Silence cuts both ways."

Artemis bowed her head, the submissive arc pleasing and useful at once.

—

She applied it to each hour like poultice.

In the kitchen she scrubbed the salt crust from the iron pot and learned how the soot slept in the corner seams.

On the gallery she swept sand and seed husks toward the ladder and learned which boards complained when touched. In the little room she mended the hem of the white skirt and learned how the window's latch sticks unless you press first, then lift. Every task was a lesson written in wood and iron.

Words were part of the house's machinery. Remove them and other parts made unaccustomed squeals. Léonie stared, thwarted of her teasing. Celeste kept glancing up as if listening for a missing bell. Baptiste looked relieved. Mère Éloise did not adjust; she had spent years speaking to things that did not waste their breath on replies.

By noon the girls had decided to test the edges of Artemis's quiet. "Tell us a story," Léonie ordered, planting herself on the gallery rail with the solemn tyranny of eleven. "How the sea tastes." When Artemis only tilted her head and smiled, Léonie huffed, slid off the rail, and ran to the blue bottle tree to clang its throats. The sound made Mère Éloise appear out of nowhere and flick the girl's ear, a neat reprimand.

"Pas de bruit," the woman said. "Don't call what you can't feed."

Silence, then, was also bait withheld. Artemis saved it like coin.

In the room of work, the chalk had been scrubbed to ghosts. Artemis knelt to pick lint from the floor and saw, near the threshold, the faintest smear of paste—herb and ash and citrus—refreshed. Later, when she carried water, she let a drop of Florida water from the bottle with the woman on it fall off the lip and run just so—neither

scrubbing nor smearing, only altering the seam's memory. A small sabotage, folded away.

At the ladder, the paste over the second rung had been renewed, green-grey as the belly of a fish. Baptiste noticed her noticing. He tugged his hat brim down. "Don't," he said.

She did not answer. She lowered her gaze as if her attention had been an accident.

"You want the boat," he said after a beat, not as accusation.

Her silence was a polite curtain. He exhaled through his nose, a tired almost-laugh. "Night wind loud tonight," he said to no one in particular. "Bottles singing. A man might hear something and walk it off." He bumped the pole with his shoulder and made it ring. "Before dawn."

Artemis dipped her head, respectful to the weather.

Baptiste touched the pirogue's tie with two fingers, then left it, as if announcing the knot and denying it in the same breath. He turned away to whittle a peg, borrowed his attention elsewhere, and left her alone with the information.

She made a kit, the way women have always made kits when departure is a kind of prayer.

Under the pallet she slid the bone spoon—an extra, not the one Celeste counted. In the hem of her shift she stitched a pinch of salt and two pins, heads east. The sailor's knife she oiled and wrapped in rag; it sat flat against her breastbone, a second sternum. She took one candle end from the shrine with a sin's neatness and left in its place the copper penny used to blind a fish's eye. From the poppet Mère Éloise had stitched, she pinched a single thread of her own hair and tucked it in the seam of her skirt. The cardman's oilskin she tied into the white skirt's waistband, the Queen of Cups and the Tower paper-thin against her hip: company, or map, or memory.

Food was trickier. Porridge did not travel. She dried two slices of bread by the kitchen stove, turning them so slowly Celeste didn't trouble to scold. They turned black at the corners. Léonie would have snatched them as a joke if she had seen; but she did not see, because Artemis lifted her eyes only when she meant someone else to look where she looked.

Water would be worst. The rain barrel had a lid that complained. The marsh would drink her if she drank it. She set that problem aside the way women set aside winter—get through the week; then turn and get through the next.

In the afternoon, wreckers again. Two pirogues slid past, loaded indecent with luck: a water keg; a length of sail; a trunk with its insides damp like a heart's. A third boat held men and no cargo, their heads bare to the sun, eyes that did not know when to be guests. One man's hat brim was curled up, river-stylish; his mouth, when it found Mère Éloise on the gallery, curled the same.

"Bonne après-midi," he called, easy.

Mère Éloise's mouth had no patience for flirt. "Afternoon," she returned, English smooth.

"You see anything come on the tide, Maman?" He did not mean a barrel.

Éloise took this sort of talk like a fly—brushed it without disgust. "I see trees," she said. "They ask for kisses." She pointed with her chin at the blue bottles. "They get them."

The boatmen laughed and did not, and moved on. Baptiste watched their backs as a hound watches men who leave their boot prints in the wrong place. Artemis watched the tie on the pirogue—old rope, new knot—and wrote it in her ledger.

Toward evening, the air grew a lid; the bottles spoke. "Wind will swerve," Baptiste said, half to the water. "Hours before dawn." He did not look at Artemis, which is a kind of looking.

Mère Éloise set her table: rum uncorked to smell, coffee poured and left to bless the air with bitterness, three slices of bread separated like well-behaved sisters. "Not a big circle," she said, almost kindly. "Just listening. We won't pull."

Artemis bent her head and kept her vow. She placed her bare feet on the cool of the chalk ghosts and offered her silence like a plate with nothing on it: if a thing came to eat, it would have to bring its own food. The hunger under her ribs rang its bell. Éloise sang. The room's temperature shifted a degree, a good dress let out one seam. Something pressed the air like a thumb on a peach, testing.

It asked, again, in that iron patience. It had tides braided into it, and driftwood, and hospital corners. It knew her name.

Artemis hid the name in the back of her tongue and put her teeth in front of it. She pictured a stone. She pictured mud. She pictured nothing, which is the hardest picture to hold. When the press became sweet and familial—*a stór, a pháiste, open the door*—she lifted the heel of her hand and pressed it into her breastbone hard enough to hurt, a human answer to an inhuman ask.

"Bien," Mère Éloise said between verses. "You do not want."

Want is a weapon; not-want is sharper. Artemis leaned into not-want until the want slid off her like a shawl a woman chooses not to wear.

The press departed without the drama of claws withdrawing. It simply was not there anymore, leaving a dent in the room that would take an hour to unspring. Éloise's song settled into work-singing—tidy, satisfied. She snuffed two candles and left one to supervise the dark.

"Tomorrow," she said, as if naming laundry. "We wash you in the lake."

Lake meant Pontchartrain. Lake meant open water, blue bottles laid flat, the city a rumour over there. Baptiste's head lifted half an inch. Celeste went still. Léonie grinned with wolfy delight.

Artemis lowered her face. Words would have broken and spilled.

She lay awake. The candle watched. The net trembled when she breathed. Frogs made their clocks; insects sawed; fish ticked. She counted boards to the door: three that complained, four that didn't. She counted breaths between the bottles' small bells. She put the white skirt on over her shift and sat down, then stood up again, rehearsing the feel of departure so her body would not balk when the hour arrived.

At the basin she rinsed her face and hands in water that remembered rain. She let three drops fall on the chalk seam by the threshold and three on the rung paste and three on her own tongue. Florida water had not been made for breaking; but it was a solvent of memory, and tonight she wanted the house to forget her in one straight line.

When the room grew the particular thinness that happens an hour before dawn, Baptiste's not-humming ceased. A quiet foot on the gallery; a notch in the night where a man turned his hat brim down. The pole kissed the pirogue's side and came to stand, listening. The bottles up-spoke once, a warning and a thank you. Wind lifted the edge of the white skirt. Artemis put her palm flat against her sternum to tell herself the knife was still there.

Celeste turned in sleep, murmured the name of a saint she could not have been taught; Léonie's arm flung out and found the wall. Mère Éloise's chair creaked, the kind of creak a woman makes when she falls asleep because other, weaker people insist on sleeping too. The candle gave a last low sigh and went out, obedient and correct. In the absolute that followed, the swamp held its breath.

Artemis rose without noise, put her foot down where the board would remember a lighter woman, and felt the chalk seam's lesson without being instructed by it. She stepped over the line, and then over the threshold penny, and then over the nail that had been upright yesterday and was sideways tonight. Silence, being her ally, did not tell on her.

She took three steps; then one more. The ladder received her feet with a small, sticky reluctance that the rain's thin memory smoothed. She slid palm to rung, rung to rail, and felt her way to the pirogue's nose where moss had been pressed—sometime this afternoon—into the creak the hull made when touched. She congratulated the person who had done it with a gratitude that did not confess.

The knot was an old friend: rabbit out the hole, round the tree, back in. She unmade it with a lover's economy. The pirogue breathed. She breathed back.

The pole was where poles are. She lifted and found it heavier than thought—wood made water-accurate. She set it and pressed and heard the mud answer like a man who does not want to move from a good chair. She pressed again and the boat slid one personal length away from the ladder and its guardian paste.

Behind her the house said nothing, which is a language too.

Artemis paused in the new dark and listened for the shape of pursuit. None came. Mère Éloise had either allowed the test or failed to wake at the invader's hour. Baptiste was somewhere being a wall. Celeste and Léonie slept with their hands open. The bottles in the

blue tree whispered to one another, catching and releasing small pieces of night.

She set the pole again. The pirogue answered. The water lifted its old hems and made room.

At the mouth of the yard, where the knees of trees mark off private from public with no fence, she drew the pole up, held it horizontal, and watched the surface until she could read it. Currents moved like snakes and were snakes. She picked the channel that smelled least of teeth. The white skirt glowed like bad moon. She pressed herself down into shadow, flattening into the boat's idea, which is: be wood; be patient.

She did not look back. The secret wants you to look back; it gets its energy that way. She counted instead— how long it took a bat to cross the same patch of air; how many heartbeats lived between pole and set; how many slow breaths one woman could take before a house remembered her weight.

When the house does, it will call. She will be where she is going to be anyway.

The swamp made a low road, a secret one. Baptiste had taught her without teaching; the water had sketched it in the muscles of her arms while she learned other lessons. She took the left channel at the leaning cypress, not because left was wise but because a vine there had broken and healed, and broken and healed; and she recognized kinship.

A splash too close punctured the grammar. She froze. Eyes like marbles slid under the boat and past, bored.

The boat did not confess her presence. When the quiet wrote itself again, she went on.

At the next bend the wind from the lake walked into the swamp, lost its hat, and laughed. It carried a rumour: tar, smoke, bread—City. Artemis's mouth filled with water she did not have. She swallowed nothing and counted. Left, then right; count of eight on a long press; count of three to fetch breath.

The pirogue nosed a stand of weed that had organized itself into a wall. She bribed it with the candle end, set carefully in the vee of a stalk as if leaving coin in a toll-house. The weed considered the etiquette and parted just enough to let a woman with a hard future through.

Behind her, the house woke wrong.

A chair scraped; a child called a name that did not belong to anyone present; the blue bottles banged their throats in angry bells. Mère Éloise said a word that was not for girls' ears. Baptiste did not shout. He does not shout. But the pirogue ties, when his hand found them, were no longer knots, and indignation is a sound even rivers recognize.

"Artémise," Mère Éloise's voice floated at last, not loud—she does not do loud—but precise as a pin. It reached the water the way her Florida water had reached the threshold: exactly, without apology.

Artemis set the pole and pushed and let the boat be her mouth.

She did not answer.

The channel narrowed, then opened. Night found room to be wide again. Stars cut small holes in the lid of the world. Ahead, a smear brighter than dark suggested lake. The air eased a fraction into cooler. Her arms shook; she forbade them. Her silence sat beside her, companionably wicked. It suggested that a woman who does not speak cannot be called back. It was lying; but it made the work lighter.

At the last knee of the last cypress, something hung that had not hung there yesterday: a pouch tied in red thread, stuffed full, still wet. Its presence scolded the branch it hung on. Artemis did not touch it. She lifted the pole, set it beyond, and let the boat pass as if she had not been seen. If it was for her, it would do its work without asking permission.

The swamp let go. The pirogue slid into a pan of water that amused the moon. The trees stopped telling her what a person should do. Far off, across a country made of black, a line of low smudges might have been the city or a trick the sky likes. Wind put its palm on her face as a mother does when a child runs too fast. She did not cry.

"Hold," she told her hands. "Hold."

They did.

She lay the pole long in the boat and took up the short paddle left loose at her feet by a friend who did not want credit. The pirogue learned her. She dipped, pulled, dipped, pulled, her breath the metronome men had told her not to listen to. The boat's nose pointed to that smear of rumour.

Behind her, from a place that could not see her but still claimed her, Mère Éloise's voice came once more, not a command now, not a curse: a benediction mispronounced into warning. "The sea gave you," she called. "The land keeps. Remember who keeps you next."

Artemis kept the words as one keeps a thorn pulled: proof of trouble solved and a reminder to wear boots next time. She did not spend her voice. She kept her map inside her teeth.

Before dawn, with the black paling, her skirt wet as if baptized against her will, she reached a seam where still water began to breathe the way a river does when it remembers leaving home. City-scent walked out to meet her: sugar burned and coffee ground, latrine and lathe, smoke in penny-feint, music the size of a child. She signed the air with her chin, the way Baptiste did to the river, and the river signed back, disinterested and immense.

She did not look over her shoulder. A kept tongue keeps a body.

The light lifted. The pirogue carried her toward the lake's open hand and the hidden mouth of a city that would swallow and save by turns. Behind her, veils shifted on the trees as if someone had passed. In front, the world did not care who she was and would therefore be honest.

Artemis counted: eight strokes, pause; six strokes, breathe; four strokes, pray nothing; two strokes, choose. Then again. Then again.

She had kept her silence. Next, she would need a voice
that knew when to bite.

"A kept tongue keeps the body."

Chapter XI – Flight

"A woman leaving is louder than thunder,
though she makes no sound at all."
— Words chalked on a levee wall, 1850

The lake was wider than her courage, yet she crossed it.

Pontchartrain spread itself under the whitening sky, a
sheet of hammered tin with the faintest ripples moving
like breath beneath linen. Artemis crouched low in the
pirogue, her hands wrapped around the short paddle,
body trembling from effort and hunger. The swamp's
thick air had fallen behind; here the wind had space to
stretch, clean and hard, sharp as new linen on a line.

Behind her, a hush too exact to be natural lingered over
the cypress knees. A hush meant listening. She did not
turn. She had learned the language of not-looking.

The city was ahead somewhere—her nose told her before
her eyes. Smoke, sugar, coffee, horse dung, yeast: a
ferment of thousands pressed close. The horizon still
lied, but the lies were sweeter now, not swamp-murk but
smudge and glimmer.

She bent to her task, paddle dipping steady, her body
remembering rhythm even when her mind failed. Eight
strokes, pause; six, breathe; four, pray nothing; two,
choose. The old counting was rope around her chest,
keeping ribs from splitting apart.

By the second hour her arms burned, shoulders ached.
She pulled the knife from her bodice and wedged it
under the thwart beside her for quick hand. The Queen
of Cups rode in her waistband, damp and curling but still
gazing outward with that serene refusal. The Tower
sagged like a warning of what had already happened.

A shape bobbed on the lake: a keg. She nosed close, considered. Fresh? No. The wood was brined; the hoops rusted. She let it pass, unwilling to waste a breath or risk the pirogue's delicate balance. Salvage could drown a woman faster than storm.

She drank a mouthful from the rain that had pooled in her canvas square. It was already warm, tinged with the faint bitterness of whatever herbs had once been steeped there. It ran down her throat like honesty, harsh and necessary.

The first pursuit announced itself not by sight but by sound: the muted slap of a paddle off-rhythm with her own. Far back. Cautious. Patient. She froze mid-stroke, let the boat drift, and listened. The hush grew teeth.

"Maman," Léonie's voice carried, small and mocking. "Elle est là."

The girl's tones floated thin, as if the swamp itself enjoyed playing ventriloquist. Artemis bent flat to the pirogue, made her body into wood, and waited.

The water lay smooth, giving nothing. She risked a glance—saw only horizon. But the voice had been real; she had heard it as sure as she had once heard Michael count his numbers wrong.

She paddled on, slower now, conserving. The pursuit would not come in haste; haste was for those who feared losing.

Toward noon clouds gathered, merciful at first—shade, reprieve—but then stacked dark and heavy, thunder muttering across the wide. The lake was no Atlantic, but it had its moods. Wind snatched the hem of her skirt and made the pirogue quiver.

She angled toward a stilted structure half-sunk, a fishing shack long abandoned. Its posts leaned, its planks gaped, but a roof still stood over half. She pulled the pirogue beneath, tied it with a woman's knot, and crouched among cobwebs and bird droppings as rain hammered down.

Lightning showed her reflection in the water, sharp and unfamiliar. A face stripped to bone and stubbornness. A mouth kept shut. Eyes that had seen storm and net and had not opened to either.

When the rain eased, she went on.

By dusk, city-scent was stronger, undeniable. The lake's far shore showed itself at last: a line of levee, docks like crooked teeth, and behind them spires and smoke. She had reached the threshold.

But thresholds are guarded.

Two men in a skiff came rowing out, eyes keen as gulls. Their hull bore no saint's paint, no fisherman's sign— wreckers turned river-rats. One called in rough French, "Femme! Where you come from?"

She dipped her head, silent, her paddle trailing as if she did not understand.

They grinned. "Wreck," one said. "Storm gave us plenty. She gave us you too."

The skiff nosed closer. Artemis felt the knife at her ribs like a friend's hand. She sat taller in the pirogue, set her face blank as stone, and let silence cloak her.

The nearer man reached. His hand brushed the gunwale—then jerked back, hissing. On the rail where her fingers had rested, a chalk line still clung, faint but faithful, brought from Éloise's house without her knowing. It had remembered its work.

The men cursed. One spat, crossed himself, and both backed water in haste. "Not ours," one muttered. "Marked." They rowed away, looking elsewhere for luck.

Artemis exhaled once, long and quiet. The chalk had saved her—Éloise's hand, unwilling to let go, or merely its own persistence? Rescue and capture. Blessing and tether. She did not untangle it now.

Night fell as she scraped the levee. The pirogue grounded in mud, the bow grating against timbers cut by men. She clambered out, legs weak, skirt sodden, knife still hidden at her breast.

Above her stretched the ramparts of New Orleans: lanterns swinging, shouts in French and English, bells tolling vespers and commerce alike. Music leaked across the water—fiddle, drum, a woman's laugh. Horses stamped on planks. Life pressed thick as yeast.

Artemis set her feet on the boards and whispered to herself, as if testing whether the name still fit in this new world:

"Artemis Danger."

The levee boards heard and did not laugh. The city waited.

She did not look back.

"Not all nets are made of rope."

Chapter XII — Wilderness Without Maps

"A person is a compass if she learns her own needle."
— From the journal of a river pilot's daughter, 1851

The levee taught her one lesson—thresholds are guarded—and the swamp taught her the rest. She did not go up into the city that first night. Lanterns swung, bells told a story in three languages, men's shouts braided and un-braided on the wind; fever flags snapped yellow along certain wharves like tongues. A watchman with a cudgel and a yawn paced the nearest ramp and spat into the river with the bored authority of a small god. Artemis stood calf-deep in mud below the timbers, eyes level with plank skirts, and found that her body refused that climb the way a body refuses a second drowning.

So she slid sideways, back along the water's edge, into the weed and cane where boards turned to silt and law turned to habit. The pirogue kissed a slick bank and grounded; she took the knife, the oilskin packet with the Queen of Cups and the Tower, the salt pouch sewn in her hem, the candle stub that smelled faintly of Éloise's house—and left the boat nudged under cane, as if tucking a child in against rain. The river breathed beside her like a sleeping animal that would not wake for her; behind her the lake breathed the same way. Between them lay the low country of neither and both—the batture—scrub and driftwood, thief-paths and washerwomen's poles, rat towns under pallets, a civilization made of refusal.

She walked. Not far; walking was a word her legs did not yet mean. She made progress in small negotiations: two dozen steps, a breath against her teeth until the knife remembered its seat at her sternum, a pause with her palm on her ribs to count them like slats. Eight, six, four, two. Begin again.

Dark laid its hand across her head. The air held heat the way cloth holds scent; it would not set her down. Insects discovered her and filed their reports with great industry. She had left the net behind with the bed and the blue bottles. Here the veil was made of hunger with wings.

A tumble of driftwood had piled itself into a suggestion of shelter where the river had thrown up the bones of older boats. She crawled into it, made a roof of two palmetto fans torn loose by some former wind, and let her spine find the old geometry of the hatch she had once married. The river muttered; the cane argued with itself; far off, the city coughed and sang. Sleep was a loan that came in small coins and had to be paid back with interest.

At dawn the light rose slow and mean, as if it had not forgiven the night for leaving. She drank the warm rain she had trapped in the palmetto's cupped hands and got grit with it, and the grit made it taste like a promise. She spit once, politely, at the ground, the way Mère Éloise had spit at the bag she tied: a punctuation, not a curse. Her mouth remained a kiln; her belly kept making its small fists and opening them again.

She took stock as a woman takes stock before washing day. One knife, mean and honest. One candle stub with a wick that remembered work. One salt pinched into the hem, two pins heads-east, a bone spoon stolen from kindness. One oilskin with a Queen who did not drown and a Tower that had already fallen. One body with a good map of hurts and a will that had not yet spent itself.

Water first. The river was a brown shoulder uninterested in being cupped. She followed a seam of ditch that smelled less of rot and more of leaf, and found where

rain had queued itself in low places. She scooped with the spoon and let it settle, then drank slow, making a ceremony of it to please her hunger with the theatre. The water had tannin in it, a tea brewed of bark and patience. It made her tongue smart. It made her kinder to herself.

Food next, or the idea of it. The shore offered shells like flint chips—oyster, broken, clean as bone. A raccoon's prints stitched the mud with clever hands. Fish had had their say and left scales like old stars. Artemis made a spear because that is what stories tell a woman to do: a stick sharpened against another stick, the edge tested against her thumb, the thing held in hand until the hand stopped being shy. She stabbed the water's eye and fetched up nothing but reflection and a memory of the cardman grinning with his singed brow: *Queen, Tower, drowning woman who does not drown.* She laughed once, a dry sound that startled a heron.

She altered the plan. She watched the raccoon's ladder of prints, followed them to a hollow log where the water made a small oratory and leaves had fallen to make a dark. She baited that shadow with a thin scab of bread she had dried by a stove yesterday afternoon, set the log's mouth in the shallows, waited. The world was not in a hurry. Toward noon two small armoured gentlemen—crawfish, furious—walked into her argument and could not find their way out again. She lifted the log, dignified as a priest with reliquaries, and knocked them into a bowl made by the palmetto fan. Their objections were noble. She apologized and boiled them in a thought—she had no pot—so instead she lit the candle and singed their whiskers with a useless tenderness and cracked their armour with a small rock until meat admitted itself. The taste was sweet and wrong and perfect. Hunger blessed it with a church's solemnity.

By afternoon the sun became a man with questions. Where were her people? Where was her plan? How long did she think to live without learning the names of every insect with a mouth? She answered with work. She plaited reed into a poor mat to lay between her ribs and the wet ground. She stitched the hem again where the pins' heads had bit through. She scraped Spanish moss from a branch and found it held more water than comfort; she wrung it into her mouth and then laid it out to answer the sun for her later. She plucked burs from her skirt and set them on a leaf like little fists and told them they had behaved badly. Her mind liked being given errands.

Signs of other people published themselves with the restraint of the poor. A shoe sole with the toes gone and the heel bitten by a dog of time. A cookpot lid that remembered soup like a rumour. Three sticks tied in a triangle and leaned against a log, which meant only what the hand that tied them had meant that day. She did not follow any path that had been made on purpose. Purpose, lately, had owned knives.

Toward evening she went looking for dry. Dry in this country was a joke told among friends. Still, she found the heartwood of a fallen cypress that had dreamt of fire when it was young. She shared it with the knife into threads and made a bird's nest of shavings in her skirt's lap. The candle stub fretted at being asked for two tasks in one day. She loved it into flame with patient cupping and the kind of breath that never once had been prayer and now could pretend, for flame's sake, to be. The shavings accepted, grudging, then earnest; a scrap of linen from her shift paid in without complaint; a stick; another; a cone of twigs; a small, grown thing.

Heat put its palm on her face. Smoke found her throat and stung and tasted like belonging. The fire was a secret made public. It would draw what it would draw. She fed it stingily and set herself to the work of not loving it too much. A woman who has been kept keeps her own leash tight.

Night pressed up against her like a cat that has decided you are furniture. Frogs did their liturgy. Far off, if far has meaning in a place where sound walks on water, she heard a drum tap out a polite argument and answer itself. Congo Square lived somewhere beyond the levee's back, a city's heartbeat drumming itself toward Sabbath or sin. She took the Queen from the oilskin and set her face-up near the fire, then turned her back on it because Léonie's voice had said, in a doorway, *Careful—things breathe when you set them like that.* The card lay there anyway, and if it breathed, it did not require her witness.

Mosquitoes made a small murder of her. She covered her arms with mud and her face with smoke and counted until counting outlasted itch. She learned the weights of dark: the quarter hour in which every piece of her remembered the Atlantic and tried to leave her mouth; the single minute after, where grief took its seat and behaved; the half hour when fear found a loose board in her chest and pried, and she nailed it back with the smallest nails, the ones you use for picture hooks. The veil of Éloise's net—chambray and charm—was not here. Only the veil made by her own stubborn breath.

She woke at a wrong angle with a different heat close to her. An animal—hog, perhaps—had come to consider the

fire and the small woman in its light. She did not start; starting is for deer. She made herself taller by half an inch, raised the knife not to strike but to declare jurisdiction, and said in the mother-tongue syllables that had never failed to make a boy pause, *No.* The animal snorted, a scholar's critique, turned, broke palmetto, and left. Her hands shook after; she laid them flat on the mat she had made and praised it for being between them and dirt.

Rain came with morning in the way of this country— sudden, warm, thorough, apologizing only with the gift it left behind. She let it fill every cup she had: shell, leaf, the spoon, even her mouth, a fool's cup but a useful one. The fire lay down without complaint and smoked itself into history. She wrapped the candle stub in oilskin and set the knife where it would dry as if it were a child's shoes.

A man crossed the batture at noon as if it belonged to him; perhaps it did. He wore a hat with a brazen curl and a face that had loved brawls more than women. He had a net over his shoulder and the shoulders for it. When he saw her—white skirt turned dun, hair hacked by fever, eyes that had learned to shut—he adjusted his stance the way men do when they mean to turn attention into property.

"Bonjour, Belle," he said, easy as small theft. "You are lost."

"I am where I am," she answered, because silence is a blade but a statement is a shield. Her voice shocked her—low and even, not obedient to the fear that had asked to borrow it.

He came two steps closer. She let the knife's handle
show itself by accident. He saw, and smiled in that way
men smile when your weapon is also their
entertainment. "I can show you a better corner," he
offered. "Food. Friend." The second word had
quotation marks you could cut your hand on.

"Merci," she said, the nice French with which women
pay the toll and keep moving, and she kept moving:
sideways, not back, keeping the river's breath to her left
and the city's cough to her right. He watched a minute
more and then shrugged and made a small decision that
had more to do with his afternoon than with mercy. He
went his way. Artemis's knees did their quiet
conversation: We will hold; we will hold.

She rested under a dock whose boards had learned a
song; the river slapped them in a rhythm men had not
asked for and used anyway. A child above somewhere
sang a line from a street song: something about a
butcher, something about a girl with apples. The words
fell through the cracks and broke on her, harmless. She
let them. The world had room for useless sound again.
This was either a gift or a trap. She decided, as she often
would now, to take it as the former until it proved itself
the latter.

Around afternoon the sky put on another hat. Wind ran
its fingers against the river's grain and made it snarl. She
gathered her rank possessions and moved inland half a
dozen yards into a little stand of saplings that had grown
insolent where men's hands were tired. There she found
a post painted white with notches cut in it—a river man's
mark, or a surveyor's, or some cousin of both.
Civilization's fingernail. She put her palm against it and

said *Hello* without voice. The wood said nothing. She
liked it for that.

Hunger bent her double by late day and she bartered
with it: ten steps, a rest; ten steps, a story she would not
tell out loud; ten steps, the taste of crawfish remembered
in a mouth already occupied with spit. In the mud a long
track wrote itself: alligator, younger than authority but
older than play. She rerouted without scolding herself
for fear. Fear, on good days, is a map.

At the day's end she set another shelter, better this time—
palmetto fans woven over a rib of driftwood, a mat like a
poor quilt between her and the worms' opinion. She
placed the Queen of Cups face-down beside her, so that
if she breathed, she would do it privately, and the Tower
face-up as if to say, *I have already paid this toll; send
your bill elsewhere.* She ate what could be called a meal
if the law allowed for kindness: two crawfish coerced into
her trap, a handful of wild onion she recognized by its
insolent stink, another spoon of tannin water made to
taste better by telling it so.

When dark came, she thought of Éloise's hands. She did
not think of the chalk on her skin. She refused to borrow
Éloise's net in her mind, because nets work even when
imagined. Instead, she counted a prayer that was not a
prayer but a list: knife, spoon, Queen, Tower, salt,
candle, breath. On *breath* she stopped and began again.

The second night was blacker. A storm beyond the lake
argued with an ocean far away and the argument came to
her only as a blue pulse in the clouds. Once, somewhere
on the river, a shot cracked and went out; once,
somewhere on the levee, a man laughed with the relief of
someone who has made it home with his body still

accommodating his names. Artemis cradled her silence and slept in patches between its paws.

Morning brought a bird with a monk's hood and a spear bill, arrogant as a clerk. It stood to the side and watched her tidy the camp, its gaze a small insult. She bowed to it. "Sir," she said, and meant it not as mockery. It hopped once and dismissed her.

She worked the little trap again and made the log argue with water until it agreed to keep what she gave it. She found a cluster of blackberries mean as gossip and bargained with their thorns. She swore softly when a briar caught the white skirt and made a new story near the hem; then she put spit on the rip and made it lie down. The trick with the candle worked again with the cypress heartwood, and this time she fed the fire not because of fear but because fire makes a mind less lonely.

She did not cry. She did not pray. She spoke aloud when necessary to keep words from rusting. "I am here," she told the post with notches when she passed it on her small patrol. "I am here," she told the river when it pretended not to know her. "I am here," she told the body that did not feel like hers yet, and the body, flattered, tried harder.

Toward evening—day three or four since the levee, time did not hold still long enough to be counted reliably—she found a sign so clean it made her knees consider giving a little: on a willow trunk at man-height, a neat blaze in the bark and below it chalk, yes chalk, a line and an arrow pointing south and a mark like a nail's head. Pilot's sign. River men who left messages for one another and for anyone clever enough to read them. Civilization's

handwriting, cursive and confident. She did not follow it. Not yet. A net can be made of guidance.

She folded herself under the palmetto that night with the Tower under her palm and the Queen under her cheek and the knife where hearts keep old letters. She dreamed of Dublin's quay for the first time since the wreck—of bales stacked like paragraphs and a gull that could not decide which language to scold in. The dream did not mourn. It catalogued. She woke with the sensation that she had put another ledger to rights.

The next day the heat stood and dared her. She dared it back. The trap pleased her with monotony. The spoon made a ceremony of water again. The onion patch forgave her its thefts. Work, repetition, small vows—all of it stitched a woman back to herself. By dusk she could say aloud the sentence she had not been allowed at sea: "I will live," and the world did not contradict her to her face.

She rose early, because men who patrol are lazier at first light, and because the sun had not yet remembered its anger. She turned her body toward the south where the pilot's chalk had pointed, and where smoke wrote readable words on the sky, and where music and fever and money and cruelty and a kindness she had not yet met waited like a table set for company. She did not think of Éloise. She did not think of the levee watchman. She thought of bread and of a bed that did not move and of a room with a door she could bar from the inside with nothing but a chair.

She went. The river to her left breathed like an old animal; the back land to her right rustled with opinions; the path under her feet declared itself in inches. She counted: eight steps, breathe; six steps, swallow; four steps, look back—no; two steps, choose. Then again.

She was not lost. Lost is a matter of ownership; the trees did not own her, only named her as she passed.

"To be lost is to be named by every tree you pass."

Chapter XIII — Hunger Teaches

"Hunger is a teacher who never wastes her words."
— Chalked on a bakery shutter after the storm, New Orleans, 1852

The morning taught her that want has timetables. It woke her before the birds, sat her upright, and put its hand under her ribs. Not cruelty—administration. She had eaten too little yesterday for the work she'd asked of the day; the day had kept its ledger and sent the bailiff at dawn.

She answered with task. It is the only answer the hungry respect.

The crawfish trap in the hollow log had been modest yesterday, comic in its small triumph. Today she made two. She found another log—shorter, sound on one end and rotted to the right softness on the other. She jammed a grate of twigs into the soft mouth, left a slit mean enough to admit vanity. A sliver of dried bread under a pebble in the back. She set the first in shadow under a willow, the second in the ditch seam where water checked and whispered. Then she turned her back on both. A watched trap is stingy.

She walked the batture slow, the river on her left like a long thought she could not be done thinking. The city made weather of its own; smells rolled out of it in tides—sugar burned to singe, fat from breakfast frying, coffee with its friendly bitterness. Heat headed for noon and the sky tried on a white that might become storm. She picked her steps through cane and drift and found a carcass—fish, a long one, gar maybe, hauled up and argued with, then forgotten. She took a moment to be honest with herself about what she was tempted to do.

Then she made a cross in the air nobody had to bless and let rot keep its promises alone.

At the first trap the log had grown heavier than law. She tipped it and caught three crawfish and a small crab with opinions. The second log held two more and a leaf that looked smug. She thanked no saint; she thanked stubbornness. The bone spoon lifted river water into the palmetto fan; she swished the creatures clean and muttered an apology they were not owed and they did not hear. She had no pot; she was not yet brave enough to eat raw. She built a small, correct fire with the patience of a woman learning stitches and set flat stones where flame could lick them and not leap. On this poor hearth she laid the crawfish. Redness rose in them like anger. She ate neat, because neatness is dignity and hunger does not get the whole of a woman.

It was not enough. The body knows.

Work then, again. She cut cane, green yet but willing, and split it with the knife into two long slats. She braided a tilt basket crude as a first prayer: a funnel where minnows might think themselves safer than they were. She dragged it into a shallow run and staked it with palmetto ribs. She crushed a handful of wild onion and smeared its insolence at the mouth. If fish liked jokes, they would enjoy it. If not—well, she admired her own industry for exactly one heartbeat and kept moving.

A print in the mud made her stop—human, barefoot, the toes strong and pragmatic. It pointed south, toward the levee, and had been made this morning. A second set joined it later, boots, heels dug in. She stepped above her own shadow. Men do not own all paths; but this one belonged to men. She peeled off longwise through cane until her skirt snagged and complained. She bent to free it with care a girl gives a hem the day she means to look like a woman. The pinheads in her seam flashed east, small stars, and made her smile like a traitor: a poor charm is still a charm.

At the white pilot post, she'd greeted yesterday she paused only to put two fingers to it. A promise: I am not forgetting you. The wood kept its silence, and she loved it better for refusing conversation.

She found a cluster of mussels like blue knuckles at the edge of a backwater, half-buried in the brag of mud. She pried two up with the spoon, freed three more with the knife's mean leverage. She knew nothing about sicknesses that ride in shellfish; she knew only that she had been hungry before and had survived by asking the world impertinent favours. She raked coals out of the small fire and set the shells in the hot like flat pots that knew their trade. They opened like men made to be honest. The meat tasted of river and iron. She ate with care and waited for harm like a patient for a name. Harm did not hurry to meet her. She wiped her mouth with the back of her wrist and nearly wept from the waste of water in the gesture.

Past noon the sun made a law about standing. Shade was no longer comfort; it was citizenship. She sat among the palmetto with her back to a log and mended the white skirt where the briar had written its sentence. The thread she used was the last of a generous length Celeste had spared, and Celeste's hand travelled with it—girl-manners, proud stitches, the little pride of making something stay together another day. Artemis tied the

knot neat and bit the end and swallowed the bit because the body likes small lies it can call food.

She kept counting—because numbers are fences and you can lean on fences. Eight breaths. Six heartbeats. Four strokes of the needle. Two looks at the river to be sure it had not decided to move the other way out of spite.

By late afternoon the funnel basket held a confession—six minnows, a frog offended, a crawfish that had not yet learned. She let the frog go with thanks and the small arrogance of a woman with better options. She ate the fish whole after they stiffened at the heat, a sin against gentility, and found herself fierce enough to enjoy it. That fierceness startled her—then pleased her—then frightened her again, as if she had borrowed a stranger's smile and found the fit too good.

Something moved in the cane with a decision, not the skitter that rats make or the delicate impatience of birds. She turned slow and found a dog the colour of swamp water looking at her as if she were a question, it had already answered twice. The body was lean as an argument; the ears had been nicked by fights or flies; the tail made no case for joy. Half-wild. Owned perhaps last year by a man who named him and then put down the name one morning and did not pick it up again.

"Sir," she said, because it is never wrong to begin with courtesy.

The dog held its ground. Its gaze slid to the fire, back to her hand, down to the bone spoon. It licked its own mouth in slow punctuation.

She kept the knife low, acceptable, admitted. "We are not enemies," she told it, the way you tell weather your plans.

It did not believe or disbelieve. It lowered itself to sit, a motion that admitted hunger without confessing need. She pulled a roast minnow from the coals and tossed it a hand-breadth short. The dog did not move until she looked away; then it stepped forward and took the offering without noise, the exact theft polite people execute at parties when they do not know how much they are owed. When she looked back, it had retreated to the same distance, the exact same pose, rigorous as a saint.

They ate in company, which is different from together. After, it stood, shook river from its coat that was not there, and left with the gravity of a judge who must go back to his court.

Hunger had, at last, sat down rather than pacing. It coiled. It watched her. It waited for tomorrow. She accepted its terms.

By evening the sky had the thick-lidded look of weather that will not become honest until the hour it has chosen. She rebuilt her poor shelter with fewer mistakes; the mat lay flatter; the palmetto inclined itself to work with her rather than against. The candle stub consented to be wick by grace, not duty, and she used its light to examine the oilskin cards. The Queen of Cups had curled but not lost her calm; the Tower had taken on a new bruise at one corner as if insulted by being made true so hard. She set them both under the lip of a board where rain, that liar, could not tempt them to swell. Then she slid the

knife under her shift, the hilt an honest weight, and lay down.

Dreams—if that is what to call them—came patient, but they came. Her mother did not preach; her father did not turn away. Michael, solemn as a clerk, counted to seventy-two and then to fifty-six and looked up, annoyed. She touched his hair as if smoothing linen on a line and woke with her hand in the air, smoothing nothing, embarrassed in the dark. She told herself aloud, to make it truer, "We are not haunted; we are hungry." The words did not mind being both.

Night tested her with sounds that demand interpretation. A hog's rooting at a respectful distance. A splash that meant a turtle tired of the day. The slow sawing breath of something larger—'gator, most likely—that had no business caring about a woman with a candle stub and a string of pins. She did not bolt. She adopted Baptiste's posture, learned first by imitation and then by bone: be a wall. It worked even when no one knelt to it.

In the hour before dawn, she discovered the lesson that made the day hers: she could make a snare good enough to hum while it waited. Not in the high brush, where laws are different and muscles stronger than hers would object—but low, along a rat-run under the drift. She unwound palmetto fibres, twisted them into cord, doubled them into a loop, tied a slip, set it where habit made a tunnel. She did not imagine catching anything noble. She wanted stubbornness that had made the mistake of routine bigger than itself. She set two snares. She left them and did not watch. She would learn nothing from watching snare or pot; you learn from

walking away and then coming back ready to be disappointed without tears. It is a marital art.

Dawn found her spooning tannin water into her mouth and pretending tea. She told herself a story she would never put in air in any room with chairs: she was a woman with a little house and an alley garden and a good kettle; she scolded bread gently for uneven rise; she sent a boy to market with a coin and a threat. She let the story warm her and then she folded it away, the way one folds the cloth over a loaf you cannot yet cut.

At the snares: one empty, smug about it; one with a rat that had strangled mid-argument, the loop working the way math works. It was a gift she did not want, given by a person she did not like, for an occasion that did not bear celebration. She took it anyway, because to refuse is to make a rule that hunger collects interest on. She skinned it with apology and the knife's mean honesty, and she roasted it hard because that is how you talk back to sickness. She ate until her belly was almost angry with her for letting joy into the house without warning. She washed her hands with sand and a mouthful of water, because there is such a thing as respect for the body that has not betrayed you lately.

The dog returned toward noon and watched her make the trap's reset with professional interest. "Inspector," she said, not unkind. It laid its chin on its paws in the universal gesture for *you're doing it wrong*. She laughed, which was wicked and light and nearly cost her the snare because laughter loosens hands. "Fine," she told the earth. "You teach me, I'll learn." She moved the loop two finger-widths to the left. The dog lifted one ear as if

marking approval. When it left, it stole nothing and
owed nothing.

Afternoon made itself heavy as a coin on the tongue. She
waded a shallow and felt river sand give like a bed where
a man has slept too long; she retreated to the bank and
wrote that down as law. She found a willow switch long
and clean and shaved its end to a point. She practiced
with it, throwing at a stump until her wrist learned that
aim is an agreement the body makes with the future. By
the fourth throw she nicked a bit of bark off; by the
eighth she put the point where her eyes had instructed it
first. She did not call it weapon. She called it
conversation.

She followed the pilot marks at last—only for a quarter-
mile. She needed the comfort without the consent. The
chalk lines, arrows, and notches made a sentence on
trunks and posts: avoid this shoal; use that bend; water
higher last run. She did not belong to men's work; she
took milk stolen and left the cream for the owners. At a
fork where the marks went right, she went left into cane
so green it almost demanded manners. Left smelled of
onion and wet sun. Right smelled of people. People—she
had decided—should be taken like medicine: only when
the fever is worse than the cure.

By evening three crawfish, two minnows, the onion
patch, and one unlucky green frog had made their
contributions to her education. She had eaten without
shaking. Her hands had stopped fluttering at sudden
noises. She had caught herself humming a piece of a
tune so small and ragged it might have been anyone's.
She had not thought of Éloise more than twice, and both

times had given the thought a chair in the corner, not the bed.

Storm teased and then refused. The first fat drops popped in dust and died with no issue. Distant thunder turned its face to the lake and spoke to it alone. She set a little row of shells to catch any insult the sky might throw; the shells were pure of intention and useless. She loved them anyway.

She slept under the new shelter as if she had purchased the bed out of her own earnings. Rats talked in the brush like old men with nothing left to prove. The river, bored, rolled over. The dog came in the dark and sat just outside the circle of her smell and kept watch and pretended not to. She did not thank it because gratitude is a leash; she let the thing be generous on its own authority.

In the narrow hour when the body thinks of dying just to see if the mind will notice, Artemis woke with the certainty that someone stood on the levee above, looking down. She lay still and made her breath the exact measure of a sleeper's. Boots scuffed; a man cleared his throat and spat. A second voice asked a question that did not belong to anyone with patience. The first answered with the shape of words that men make when they do not want the dark to remember them. The boots went away. She did not unclench for a hundred counts.

Dawn was almost kind. The air felt washed, though nothing had washed it. She rose with a thief's stretch; took inventory in a voice you could hear from the far side of a prayer: "One woman. One knife. One spoon. One net made of patience. One dog if he decides to be." The dog lifted its head at the last and declined comment.

"One city," she added, and it felt like blasphemy and like bread.

She followed, for real now, the chalk that meant men had not merely survived here but had agreed to do it together. A white blaze; a notch; a nail head drawn in dust; an arrow pointing toward a stand of willow where the ground rose by inches and would not drown you if you slept badly. A pilot had marked this for other pilots; she was neither; she took the gift anyway and set her jaw against the debt.

At the willow she found a rag of blue cloth tied high, stiff with old weather. It reminded her of Éloise without yanking. She tied a strand of grass opposite—no colour, no claim—just to feel the knot slide. Then she walked on.

Wilderness had not ended; it had adjusted its terms. The city's breath was on her face; the river's shoulder brushed her sleeve. People happened nearer by accident. Voices came out of the cane not looking for anyone in particular. A boy laughed as if he had never been corrected. Hammer on plank spoke in the sharp code of men who intend to be paid. The world did not yet need Artemis Danger; this was a mercy. She would make it need her later.

At noon she came on a hulk of a flatboat dragged high and left for shade. A woman had made a kitchen beneath it: pit fire, a kettle with half a bottom saved for something clever, hooks in a beam for hanging fish. The place smelled of sassafras and caution. Nobody was home. She did not step under the boat. She put the bone spoon on a beam inside with its bowl facing east— what women do for one another when they can spare a blessing—and kept going.

Toward evening, she met the dog again on the path, or it met her. They walked shoulder to shadow without lie. It peeled off toward the levee with the casualness of a man who has remembered an appointment. She let it go. People think they own the dogs they feed; dogs know better. She hoped she was learning from better teachers now.

Hunger had stopped scolding. It had taken up a chair and a ledger and asked only that she keep accounting. She did.

Night gathered. The last light made the river's back look like hammered pewter; beyond, the city cracked its knuckles. She set her trap and her snare and her palate and laid the Queen face-down, the Tower face-up, the knife under her tongue in metaphor only, because metaphors are good for the courage and terrible for the gums. She slept, not as a child or a casualty, but as a worker in a bed she had earned.

In the night a job announced itself—a bigger one than snare or trap or onion patch. Not with voices, not with drums. With a breeze that smelled of yeast and iron, carrying the clatter of wheels on plank and the creak of a cart whose driver sang off-key but with belief. The city was closer; it would want her name and bargain for it. Hunger, who had taught her book-keeping, would be her advocate at the table: buy low, sell dear, don't give yourself away.

She turned on her mat without apology and gave tomorrow her back. Her last thought before sleep set its name to the page was simple and free of decoration:

I will not be anyone's kept thing again.

The river approved by refusing to answer.

"Hunger is a teacher who never wastes her words."

Chapter XIV — Fire and Ghosts

The third night came with air that smelled of rain but gave none. Her body had learned to live lean, but it still asked for bread the way a widow asks for letters: hopeless, habitual. Hunger had quieted into an overseer who checked her tally without cruelty. Still, her hands shook when she gathered driftwood.

She shaved cypress heartwood again, set the candle stub to its task, and coaxed a thin flame until it believed itself. This time the fire caught faster, a student who had been scolded yesterday. She fed it slivers, then sticks, then one proud branch. It rose, crackled, and showed her face back to her in yellow. For a moment, she felt taller than her hunger.

The warmth touched her bones like kindness. Smoke sent mosquitoes packing, at least for a while. She sat cross-legged before it with the knife across her knees and allowed herself the heresy of a smile.

But fire announces itself.

From the cane came rustle, footfall—not hog or dog this time, but human, cautious. Artemis froze. Shadows moved beyond the fire's reach. She tightened her hand on the knife and leaned her shoulder until her profile became part of a stump.

"Who's there?" she called, voice even, low, as if she owned the ground.

Silence answered. Then a mutter, two syllables in French, swallowed by the dark. A man or two, watching. Waiting. Wreckers, perhaps, sniffing out what the lake had failed to give them.

She did not rise. To rise is to admit alarm. She fed another stick into the fire, slow, deliberate, as though her visitors were no more troubling than smoke. After a while the dark gave up its watchers. Branches cracked receding. The swamp reasserted its chorus.

Alone again, she breathed in a long thread, let it out slow, and laughed under her teeth. The laugh belonged to survival, not to joy.

That night, the ghosts pressed closer.

She dreamed not of the sea but of Ireland. Fields brittle with famine, rows of women bent double, their skirts heavy with mud and children both. Her mother kneading air where no flour had been, fists moving in a rhythm that remembered plenty. A cart creaking past with six coffins stacked and one child crying among them, not yet learned enough to be quiet.

In the dream she reached out, her hands sticky with crawfish juice and soot, and the child looked up with Michael's eyes.

"Seventy-two," he said solemnly, counting his fingers. "Fifty-six. Seventy-two. You never keep the line right."

She woke with tears and smoke streaking her cheeks, the fire low, the Queen of Cups face-down beside her. The Tower grinned up, blackened at the corner.

She whispered aloud, to make the sentence honest: "I am not haunted; I am alive."

The swamp disagreed, but softly.

By day she set snares and checked her fish-funnel. By noon she had crawfish enough for broth if broth were possible, which it was not. She crushed onion leaves for flavour and roasted what she could. The dog returned, patient, sitting at his distance. She tossed him a claw. He accepted, grave. Companionship, like survival, was made of scraps.

She built another fire that evening, knowing she risked notice but needing warmth. The air had teeth now; damp rose from the river with a mean chill. She fed the flame carefully, made it low, laid driftwood like modesty.

At the edge of the firelight her dead came again. The Cornishman, pipe smoke curling from a mouth no longer breathing. The aunt's hand, crooked with labour, raised in small farewell. Michael's cap, forever too large, shading eyes that would not age.

Artemis pressed her palms together, not prayer, but pressure to keep the bones in place. "Not now," she told them. "If I live, I'll remember. If I die, I'll meet you. But not here. Not in this place."

The fire cracked, and for a moment she thought it had agreed.

Toward midnight another noise came—hooves on the levee above, the sharp cadence of men on horseback. Voices, French mixed with English, carried down. One shouted about fever wards, another about salvage rights. Lanterns swung like restless stars.

Artemis shrank back, drew her fire low with sand, and wrapped herself in the white skirt. To be seen now was to be claimed. Claimed meant kept. Kept meant silence again, but not hers.

The men passed. The swamp swallowed their echoes. The dog, at his post, huffed once as if to say: *Good choice.*

At dawn she rose. The fire had burned to bone-ash, grey and delicate. She smeared it, scattered it, left no shrine behind. Ghosts travel in ashes. She would not give them the map.

The willow blaze appeared again, clearer in morning light. Beyond it, the air smelled of bread rising, sugar browning, horses sweating. The city.

Her body was failing—thin, raw, lips cracked again. But her silence had hardened into tool, her hunger into compass. She adjusted her knife at her breastbone, shouldered her poor bundle, and stepped south.

Every tree named her as she passed. She let them. She was more than their naming.

"A spark may be warmth, or a beacon, or a snare."

Chapter XV — Toward the City

"Follow the water that knows men's names."
— Note in a pilot's pocketbook, 1852

The chalk made a sentence and she obeyed its grammar. White blazes on willow and cypress, a nail-head sketched in charcoal, an arrow shaved into bark—pilot marks, river men leaving bread crumbs for each other at flood and fall. The air had changed its mind; it smelled of yeast and iron, of horses and coffee and a sweetness that was not bloom but sugar trying to become money. The city was no longer rumour. It breathed.

Artemis rose from her poor shelter before true light and set her body to the old arithmetic: eight steps, breathe; six, swallow; four, look; two, choose. Her legs had learned resignation, then obedience, then something like loyalty. She followed the marks not as a subject but as a guest; men had written them, but water had edited.

A heron, tall as a thought you cannot finish, lifted from the ditch and scolded her for needing a path. A vulture turned once above, considering; it declined to invest. The dog came and went without explanation, a grey-brown courier between worlds. When he walked beside her, they shared a silence that did not need phrase. When he left, she did not call. Anyone you can call back is also someone who can be called away.

Along the batture children's voices carried, city-proud and river-tuned—the brag of boys testing a raft, the high flute of a girl's laugh, a baby's grievance aired to the general assembly of morning. The levee above held its spine straight under carts and feet. Fever flags— yellow as a bruise becoming old—snapped on two docks, warning as only cloth can: don't come, don't stay, don't breathe too near us. Bells from somewhere Catholic tolled not sorrow but schedule. She counted them to steal an extra swallow between numbers.

Her kit was lighter than hope. Knife, bone spoon, salt stitched and two pins heads-east; candle stub; oilskin with the Queen and the Tower. The Queen's face was now worn to a suggestion—you could believe you had imagined her serenity. The Tower kept its corner bruise like the proud scar of a man who has told a story too often and still believes it.

Water first. She let dew have her cupped hands and then drank from a tannin pool where willow leaves wrote their own names and forgot them. The taste of bark and patience scolded her tongue. She broke one of her last bread-ends and held it against her palate until it gave up its ghost into spit. The dog took the other end in the decent way—when she had turned her head.

The marks took her off the open river where men had rights and into the old threads—little runs and ditches the pilots knew better than their wives' tempers. She waded twice, the water risen to knee and then to mid-thigh, skirt clinging like a child who does not want to be put down. She kept the knife high, the cards higher. Mud made its good argument that all things end here if not persuaded otherwise; she persuaded it with patience, not force. When she came up on sugarcane— row after row like soldiers that had forgotten why they stood—she knew she had crossed a line. Wilderness still spoke, but now in a dialect that men interrupted often.

The first person she saw was a woman beating a rug so fiercely it might confess. The gallery she stood on was

plank and shade and a blue bottle tree chimed along its edge like little throats. The woman paused, took the measure of the figure slanting through cane and ditch, and lifted her chin. Artemis lifted a hand, not too high—half a greeting, half a proof of emptiness. The woman looked to the inside of the house, weighed what she saw there, weighed Artemis's white skirt turned dun, the careful way a knife makes a second breastbone, and chose to return to her rug. Not cruelty. Economy.

She passed a stand of figs with leaves like hands. The fruit had not decided yet. She did not trespass. The chalk said south; she went south. At a bend a plank bridge had been thrown together with hope and three nails; it called itself a road the way a boy calls himself a man when he borrows his father's hat. She crossed one foot at a time, her weight a whisper. On the other side a fence made of promise and palmetto attempted neatness around a truck patch: okra spears, beans on strings, greens fattening themselves on this unholy air. A scarecrow wore a gentleman's hat with its brim curled river-fashion. The dog took exception to the scarecrow and then apologized to Artemis by refusing to look at it.

Toward noon the marks gathered like a choir: five in quick time—blaze, nail, arrow, chalk line, notch— pointing left. She obeyed. The ground lifted by inches. Cypress knees withdrew their accusations. The ditch water cleared to the colour of tea well managed. A smell of bread bullied everything else for a quarter mile. She laughed once, which was wicked and costly and necessary, and pressed her hand against her ribs to keep the laughter from stealing what breath belonged to work.

A barge grated the levee, men shouting in French and English, in Irish too—a rasp in it that was home and not-home, hunger with the coat of wages on. She stepped back into cane, lowered her head, and let them be men without being herself a woman who could be counted in their number. A boy's face flashed through the slats of cargo, freckled, new, the wrong size between childhood and whatever came next. He looked and did not see. The gift of being invisible was bought dear; she spent it carefully.

Heat put its weight on everything. She rested where a sycamore made dots of shade like a dress that had been pricked for a seamstress's lesson. The dog lay with his tongue out, too dignified to pant until he had her permission; she granted it and he pretended not to take it. She dipped the bone spoon into a puddle and let the sun cook what it couldn't kill. The spoon had become a priest in this parish; everything came to its lip and was blessed as enough.

Afternoon pushed. Time became long rope; she moved hand-to-hand along it. The chalk went stingier, then generous again—the pilot who had left this paragraph had been interrupted by rain, by rum, by love, by work; she thanked him for the fragments that remained and did not scold him for the missing words. She passed a live-oak whose roots had learned to hold up a small chapel of earth; candles had been burned there before rain instructed them to stop. Someone had left a red thread tied around a nail. She touched nothing. She had been kept; she would not be marked again by accident.

Past the chapel a narrow road proper declared itself—a two-wheeled insistence through cane and willow, old ruts holding water, new ruts holding promise. A cart

had passed this morning; manure and mint had agreed somewhere along its route to share their smell. She stepped onto the road and let it name her traveller.

The road rose to the levee. She climbed halfway and crouched, the way a hare does when it has business in a world that does not vote on hares. Over the crown: the wide, brown river fat with story; flatboats bargaining with current; a long low steamer shouldering downstream as if it had invented motion. Beyond, the city lifting her roofs and her saints and her smoke and her shouts. A fever cart rolled along a street visible through the gap between two warehouses—yellow flag on the shaft, wheels telling the truth without malice.

Not yet, she told her legs. Not yet. Doors are as dangerous as hunger. She went along the levee halfway down its inside face, out of sight of men who owned hats and time. Music found her even here—fiddle, drum, a voice not singing words so much as insisting that breath could be shaped into better use than fear. Congo Square would be there, somewhere beyond the promise of the cathedral, where Sunday would turn to currency and spirit both. The thought made her scalp tighten and her feet hurry without being asked.

She came to a drainage cut—black water doing its law work, dragging the country's sins toward lake or river depending on what argument the day was having. The pilot marks pointed across. No bridge; a throw of pallets met in the middle and took pride in calling itself safe. Her body debated and then voted: yes. She balanced with the knife across her palms like a blessing or a blame and went foot, foot, foot until she was in the middle where neither bank had much claim. The pallet

made a noise like a lie. She swayed, counted, chose—
and made it.

On the far bank the ground changed underfoot—a
firmness that did not need to be wrung before it would
hold you. Truck farms had made their case here years
ago and had won; rows laid on a bias, tidy furrows, a
bucket forgotten where someone had been called to
door or bed or grief. A hoop of willow hung on a nail to
keep time. A shed leaned into its own shadow but
would not yet fall. The world had edges again.

Her body had been trading small coins all day; it
presented the bill. Knees that had carried the Atlantic
and the swamp and the levee now made a petition: stop.
She granted nothing. She went twenty steps farther to a
row of cabbages with leaves that looked like the skirts
of women who had run from a dance. She meant to lay
her hand on one—not to take, not to bruise, only to
touch something that had chosen to live in rows. Her
hand missed by an inch and found dirt. The ground
received her head with a dull generosity. The dog,
shocked out of his municipal dignity, barked once as if
to file an appeal. Darkness did its kind work.

Time left the room and returned with guests. The first
guest was the river: she could hear it deciding things
without her. The second was a wheel: it squeaked, then
stopped, then squeaked closer, then did not squeak at all
because someone had lifted the shafts to avoid waking
those who ought to wake themselves. A man spoke the
way careful men do when they are talking to animals or
the very sick.

"Easy there, now."

Not to her. To the wheel. To the day.

Hands tried her name on without asking for it: fingers at the wrist where pulse argues, the back of the other hand laid to her cheek to learn whether the fire had taken room there without paying rent. The voice again, nearer, the throat cleared after the proper hello to himself.

"Girl." A pause that did not hurry. "Girl, can you hear?"

She could not afford the word *yes* and the word *no* was too expensive. She moved a lip. The dog huffed as if translating.

"Ah," the man said, which has meanings enough to furnish a household. "You got yourself to the right side of the field, anyway."

He lifted her with the competence of someone who had carried sacks and men and babies and elder kin and had not broken in the doing. He smelled of soap made from things that had been forgiven, of coffee burned once already today and surprised to be asked for another hour, of wood-planed and planed again to fit. A cart creaked and accepted her weight. The dog jumped in without permission, then made his face blank to argue he had been invited.

The wheel squeaked politely and then consented to be quiet. The man clucked to the old mule as if to a friend who forgets his temper and remembers it. The world tilted; the cabbages passed behind; the pilot marks, for once, had nothing to say.

Artemis tried to open her eyes. One obliged and found the man's profile—a nose like a chisel, hair that had argued with hats, a jaw that entertained humour and sorrow in equal shifts. He wore no fever flag. He wore a shirt that had been laundered by hands that loved their work. He did not look at her again; he looked where the cart was going.

"Almost," he told the mule. "Almost now."

She let the cart do the counting for her. Eight jounces until a gate; six until a rail lifted; four until the shade of a gallery laid itself over her like a better version of the skirt; two until boards that remembered feet decided to remember hers. A couch or a pallet had been placed with ambition near a window that made a promise about air. He set her there with the ceremonial economy of a man laying down an instrument he intends to play again after supper.

"Water," he said aloud, which wakes a house quicker than a bell. Another voice answered—woman, older, the sound a broom makes when it is proud of its work. Footsteps argued with themselves and then agreed. A basin arrived. A cloth remembered grace. Cool touched her mouth and then her hairline and then the pulse at the neck where life has quarters. The dog took his post under the pallet as if petitions could be received there.

"Name?" the man asked. He had given none of his own. Fair dealing.

Her mouth learned its job slowly. She tried *Girl* and then *No one* and then the truth, speaker-quiet, stubborn as salt.

"Artemis," she said. The last name arrived after a pause in which the room made room for it. "Danger."

He accepted the sentence as if it were a list of tools, he would need to mend a door. "All right, Miss Danger," he said. "We'll keep you from the sun till you can keep yourself."

Keep. A word she had come to distrust. It did not hurt her now. It did not comfort. It sat between them on the air like a chair no one would take until the other had been seated.

She slept there as if the bed had grown around her to prevent her leaving, which is either mercy or strategy; her body did not file a complaint. The last thing she knew was the sound of a kettle that had opinions; the last sight, the square of window showing a wedge of sky that had finally decided to be blue.

The city had not swallowed her yet. The wilderness had led her to a door and then, mannerly, had taken itself outside.

"Every wilderness ends at a door, though you may crawl to reach it."

Chapter XVI — The Kind Old Man

"Kindness is a rope: you can be pulled to shore, or bound."
— From a washerwoman's catechism, Tremé, 1852

The room had been built to let air argue its way through. A tall window faced a yard where fig leaves laid green hands over the light. A fan—hand-made, palm plaited and looped to a nail—hung above and swung when the wind remembered. The pallet was a narrow appointment of ticking and stubbornness; the sheet smelled of lye and line-dried sun. When Artemis woke, the city was a long murmur at the sill: cart wheels over planks, a mule explaining its opinion to a boy, somebody selling something sweet in a voice that had practiced yeses and noes for money.

She tried to sit and the room explained that sitting was a negotiation, not a right. Her body was a list of invoices. The good news: breath behaved. The better news: no salt in her mouth, no swing of deck under the bones.

A woman came first—hair in a knot like a strict aunt's, dress plain, sleeves rolled. She had the look of someone who had spent her grief already and kept the folded receipt in her bodice for reference. "Voilà," she said softly, not to be pretty but because the word fit. "Eyes open."

Artemis tried her own voice and found it present, if hoarse. "Where am I?"

"In my brother's house," the woman said, offering water in a glass thick as truth. "In Tremé, near Rampart. We are not the best street and not the worst. Drink slow."

The water was cool, and if it carried a ghost of iron from the pump handle, it wore that ghost modestly. Artemis obeyed slow like a sacrament. The woman dabbed Artemis's brow with a cloth that carried a whisper of Florida water and camphor. The smell made the membranes of memory flutter—the lake, Éloise's thumb pressing a charm into the floorboards—but the room itself argued a different doctrine: chairs, wood shavings, coffee talking low in another room.

"Madame..." Artemis began.

"Not madame. Agnès," the woman said. "If you call me *Tante*, I will not stop you. He—" She tilted her chin toward the other room. "He is Gabriel. He found you in the cabbages being a fool about standing up when falling down would do."

As if summoned by the gentle insult, Gabriel came to the door with a cup in his big hand and a carpenter's pencil tucked above his ear. The light from the window wrote a new line across the chisel of his nose. He had shaved badly and did not apologize. "Miss Danger," he said, the name respectful but not precious. "Mornings are for living. Let's keep you at it."

She sat up another inch to make room for the cup. Coffee—burned a little, honest, softened by a spoon's worth of milk that had been a fight to find this morning. He watched her drink the first swallow and relaxed as if boards had fit at last. The dog, who had installed himself beneath the pallet as if it were a post in need of guarding, thumped his tail twice at Gabriel and then pretended he had not.

"You let that animal into my clean house," Agnès told her brother without fire.

"He let himself," Gabriel answered, which was the city's logic and perhaps the Lord's. He crouched—his knees complained and he ignored them—and slid a palm under the pallet to rub the dog's head. "City gave him no name he likes. He'll keep this one if he means to."

"He's called Moss," Artemis said before she could stop. She heard the syllable leave her like a card played low. The dog accepted or did not; his eyes remained the colour of swamp water explaining itself to no one.

"Moss," Gabriel repeated, not to name but to agree. He set the cup on the windowsill, where the stain of other cups made a ledger of mornings. "You've earned three more days of bed, then we turn you into someone ambulant. You don't have fever smell, thanks to God or your own stubbornness. We'll put broth in you and wood under your hands. Do you work wood?"

"I work whatever doesn't argue me into the ground," Artemis said. The answer surprised her; it pleased Gabriel.

Agnès crossed herself—not display, duty—and added, "And church if you mean to stay. Even the bad men go sometimes. It instructs the day to behave. Eat first; amend your soul second. Gabriel, leave her to me."

He did, by inches—the way men who have built chairs and coffins and suffered both learn to go. He glanced once toward Artemis's throat as if listening for a pulse and then toward the window as if checking weather on her behalf. He stood, his back hinted at old debts paid in

labour, and said, "There's a bench out back; when your legs answer you, you sit there. It's the law of the house. Sitting inside too much makes people talk like shadows." He left the room quieter and better-built than he had found it.

Agnès set broth in a blue-white bowl—the same temper as the bowl Éloise had used, but this flavour had vegetables and the thrift of bones worked twice, the scent of bay leaves and a patience learned from markets. "Small," Agnès said, handing her a spoon. "If you eat like a field hand now, your belly will write me a complaint and I will return it stamped *true*."

Artemis bent to the work of small. The spoon was a tin cousin of the bone one in her bundle. She watched her hand make the trip from bowl to mouth and remembered, without needing to expose the memory to air, the ship, the hatch, the counting. Agnès saw some of this travel across Artemis's face and patted her shoulder—not soft, correct. "We all come here by water," she said. "Some of us let the water speak for us too long."

"Your brother... is a carpenter?" Artemis asked between obedient mouthfuls.

"A joiner," Agnès corrected without arrogance. "Doors, cabinets, coffins if the fever asks impolite. He'll put a floor in a house that insists on sinking. He's a man learned by wood and by women who told him when to stop. He is a widower and not the kind that wanders. He has more patience than most saints I've had cause to thank. He is soft about dogs and children and fools. He smells of planed cypress and coffee and the rain when it becomes someone else's problem." She smiled with one side of her mouth; family affection is a language that needs no preacher. "He found you and acted as if the day had merely told him to fetch a board."

The broth disappeared while they were speaking, as if politeness had eaten it on Artemis's behalf. Agnès refilled the bowl halfway and clucked when Artemis blinked. "Do not apologize for being saved," she advised. "It offends the kitchen."

The window told on the city without being asked: a praline woman calling *Pralines, belles pralines!* in a cadence as practiced as Scripture; a pair of fiddles sparring in someone's yard; a hammer regulating a plank; French and English stepping over each other without saying *pardon*. Bells to the east, not sorrow but hours—they counted nine and she stole their numbers and made them breath.

By noon she could sit, with a mutiny enacted by the muscles of the back and then put down by reason. Agnès argued the pillow into the small of her and the world learned its angles anew. The dog shifted his post to better see both door and woman, as if promoted. Artemis put her hand to her bodice reflexively, glad and abashed to feel the knife lying flat as a second sternum. The oilskin cards remained tied into the skirt's waistband where she had slept on them as if they were bones, she dared not let the earth forget.

"You'll keep your things," Agnès said, catching the gesture without remarking on content. "We keep no one's soul in this house, only their cups. When the fever takes, those go to the poor. That is the rule." She stood, wiped her hands in her apron, and added, "If the priest

comes by, you are not obliged to give him two names. One is enough until a person belongs to their bed."

"I will give mine," Artemis said, and felt the simple pride of speaking it without somebody else's permission. "Artemis Danger."

"Bon nom," Agnès said, amused, a woman who had filed better and worse under that rubric. "We will see what it chooses for life to mean in it."

Gabriel's house had been laid out for work: a front room that did not think it was formal; a long table that understood the weight of bread; doors doubled to make air learn manners; a workshop opening on the yard where wood shavings drifted like faithless snow. In the afternoon, when Artemis's legs signed a contract for thirty steps from bed to bench, she learned the place by the soles of her feet.

Gabriel was at his bench with a plane and a length of cypress, the blade set to bite a proud hair at a time. Each stroke sang low, like a man satisfied with the topic he'd chosen. Curled shavings fell, light enough to make a poet of the air, and lay in drifts the colour of bread crust. The smell made a parable of patience. He looked up and did not make a fuss, which is its own kind of welcome; he nodded at the yard's bench, set under fig and close enough to the shop door that the two rooms could talk.

She sat. The bench had been planned into generosity by other backsides. The fig threw light back on itself; a blue bottle chimed once where Agnès had hung a string of them to catch bad luck and flies. Children clattered past the alley mouth; someone practiced a drum on a barrel with hands that had not yet met ceremony. Across the

fence a neighbour burned coffee dark enough to scold angels.

"Put your fingers here," Gabriel said, after a while, offering the plank's edge. He ran the plane; the wood warmed and smoothed under her fingers the way a river stone learns a thumb. "That is how it's meant to feel when you are done."

She obliged, and the board answered her politely. The feeling went into her hands and then up, through the bones of the arm and the hinge of the shoulder, until it altered the way her back was willing to be a person. "Don't fight grain," Gabriel said. "Learn it. You fight a man; you learn a board." He handed her a scrap and a bit of paper rough as honest advice. "Sand. Not fast. Counting helps."

Artemis obeyed and counted low. One, two, three, four—breathe. Six, eight—lift. His breathing and the plane's and hers made a small choir. Moss took a supervisory post where he could see the street and the yard both and declined to offer feedback.

"Why *Danger*?" Gabriel asked at last, quiet enough that she could pretend he had been speaking to the wood.

"Because my father's father made a mistake in a clerk's ear," she said. "And because the sea thought to swallow me and did not." She did not embroider. He has a good ear; he would hear what had not been said.

He nodded as if she had told him where the joist lay. "All right."

Agnès brought bread and a smear of something that had the decency to pretend butter and insisted that this was not dinner, merely instruction for the mouth. Artemis ate without hurry; the way women do when they mean to have work later. She asked with her eyes whether she should help with the washing; Agnès answered with hers that if Artemis stood up in that tub the neighbourhood would have opinion enough to fill the room, and she would keep the soap to herself, merci.

Gabriel spoke of the city the way a man speaks of his mule—affection lined with realism. "There are people worth your name in it," he said. "There are men who will sell you your own hands. Fever has manners only some years. The river hates and loves both because it does not know how to do one thing at a time."

"And work?" Artemis asked.

He smiled with his jaw. "Work is everywhere because laziness is the majority religion. Can you sew that skirt into something the street won't whisper at? Agnès knows a woman off St. Philip—Madame Riviere—who takes in fine work for ladies and coarse work for everyone else. Or the market: coffee stalls need hands that count and pour; laundries need backs; hospitals need women who can watch breath and not panic; kitchens always want arms that lift and do not talk. If you choose streets, choose them with a purpose. Tremé will not let you starve if you behave; the Quarter will let you be murdered if you blink."

His fairness made a shelter. She set it like a hat on her head to see if it would suit.

"And church?" Agnès added, from the doorway, uninvited in the manner of sisters. "St. Augustine is at the corner. If you cannot keep your head up without staring at God at least once a month, the ladies will figure you for proud. If you are proud, disguise it as gratitude for the weather."

"I will go," Artemis said, because she meant to take whatever shelter could be had cheaply.

"Do not kiss the priest's hand," Agnès advised. "He may think himself an emperor if you do, and then he will ask for your ears next."

The dog sneezed as if to agree that priests and fleas share an enthusiasm for ownership.

As the day unspooled, the house taught her more grammar. The water barrel in the yard had a lid that stuck unless you pressed first—like the window's latch in Éloise's room—only this was an honest stick, not a charm. The back steps sang two specific notes under a heel; Agnès stepped to avoid them with a ballerina's contempt. A neighbour's rooster was of the opinion that afternoon was morning. A boy practiced spelling *Louisiane* wrong and then right; a woman across the alley coughed the cough that would send Gabriel to his lumber rack for planks cut to size. A boy ran past barefoot with a hoop; he tripped; he did not cry; he checked whether anyone had seen; he proceeded to laugh loud enough to preserve his reputation.

"Why did you stop?" Gabriel asked when her sanding slowed. She had, without tracking it, been listening too tenderly to the cough across the alley.

"Because wood knows when men will need boxes," she said before her etiquette could correct her.

He looked at her, properly now, not with a craftsman's glance but as a man says hello to another traveller over bread. "Yes," he said. "No need to be polite about it. We sell our hands to sorrow; sorrow pays fast." He set his plane with a different bite, harder, a choice to work a knot through rather than go around. "When fever comes this year, we will not pretend it won't. Agnès keeps vinegar and lemon peels and a razor for hair. We say we do not know if these things help, and we do them anyway. That is the whole catechism."

"I know how to sit with breath," Artemis said, and surprised herself again. "I can count for someone when they are not able, until they are."

"You'll be hired just for that," he said. "Hospitals pay in currency and thanks and sometimes in death. Riviere pays in coin and needles. The market pays in gossip and coffee. Choose which religion suits you."

"Counting is mine," she said.

"Then count," he said, and returned to the plane.

Evening drew the map of Tremé in ordinary miracles: a horn somewhere, no one about to name it; drums off Congo Square, small tonight and decent; a child in the alley being called in three languages and ignoring all, which is proof of life. Agnès ladled rice and beans into bowls and pretended that salt pork was not so scarce; she set a third bowl on the floor as if the dog's manners had been proven and rescinded in one gesture. He ate with a solemnity that asked for no commendation.

Gabriel said grace as a man sets a level on a board—
briefly, with respect for the instrument and not much
ceremony. Agnès added a word for the drowned.
Artemis lowered her head and did something with her
throat that might have been prayer if any priest would
have recognized it; she kept the names behind her teeth
where they could not be stolen.

After the dishes and the small war with the pan, Artemis
stood in the doorway to the yard and watched the sky
decide whether to sleep. The wind dragged a lace of
cloud off the levee and left it snagged on a roof's nail.
The blue bottles chimed once like a polite guest. She felt
the chalk traced in Éloise's house stirring faintly under
her skin, as if charm remembered its address. She
pressed her palm flat to her sternum, not to deny it, not
to welcome—simply to own the ground where she stood.

"You're safe enough under this roof," Gabriel said
behind her, as if he had read the motion and not the
thought. "Not forever. For now." He laid a hand on the
doorjamb the way a man claims nothing but its tendency
to remain upright. "And when you leave, make it your
notion, not the city's."

She nodded, grateful for the exactness. "I will pay for the
pallet," she said. "In sanding, in sweeping, in carrying
wood, in sitting with breath if the neighbour's cough gets
ideas."

"Pay in all of it," Agnès answered, approving. "And keep
a corner of yourself unspent. City takes everything
offered. It is your job to be stingy."

They let her be alone then without making a show of it.
She stepped into the little washroom, stripped the white

skirt and rinsed it, wrung it with hands that had learned laundry from a river older than any church; the water ran brown, then less brown, then almost-honest. She washed her hair and found where Celeste's scissors had made their neat absence. She slept after with the knife under the pallet board, the oilskin under her cheek, the dog lengthwise along the underside of the bed like a beam, and did not once wake to count the ghosts as they passed. Perhaps they were tired. Perhaps they had learned her new address and were chewing it over.

Sometime well after midnight she woke to the rain, she had wanted all day, decent and heavy, steady as a rehearsal. The city accepted it with grace and a little theatre—gutters clapping, cisterns glad. She lay in the cool and let gratitude be bodily rather than theological. The roof held. The window breathed. The world continued... Morning came with bread carts and a woman calling *Calas, calas!* with a song in it and a pot of oil's promise. Agnès's broom wrote its lines across the floor. Gabriel's plane argued with a new board. The dog trotted out to examine rain's opinion of the yard and returned without commenting.

Artemis stood, counted the boards that groaned underfoot, and found she could pick which ones to spare. She went to the bench as instructed by the law of the house, set her hands to the sandpaper and the edge, and took the board a fraction closer to the version of itself it had always meant to be.

She was not kept. She was kept *for now.* It is an important difference.

"Kindness keeps for a while; courage keeps the rest."

Chapter XVII — Lessons in Doors

*"Walk as if the street already knows you,
and it will decide more gently whether to refuse."*
— From a peddler's sayings, Rampart Street, 1852

The house taught her first; the city would wait its turn. Morning was a grammar: Gabriel's plane talking low to cypress; Agnès's broom writing its curt script; the dog's patrol stitched from door to yard to gate and back, a hem kept even. Artemis learned to rise with the coffee man's call and to sit the lawful ten minutes on the bench under the fig before asking her legs for any heroics. Ten minutes for the city to smell her, ten for her to smell it back—yeast and iron and oranges bruised in a woman's apron.

"Doors," Gabriel said, on the second day she managed the bench without the light going away in a dramatist's faint. "A city is only doors. See who stands in them, whose thresholds are swept, which steps have been sat on so long they learned the shape of a woman. Count doors; you'll know more than a priest."

She counted because counting had once tethered her to a plank in an unkind ocean. Doors this time: eight along their street, each with a mouth's opinion. At the ninth, a barber's pole turned like a thought that refused to quit; at the tenth, a small shop whose window held a saint with tin rays and a sugar cone that glittered like winter. At the eleventh, Madame Riviere stood in the jamb with pins in her mouth and a yard of pale muslin over her arm, examining a client's figure as if the woman were a problem good pinning could solve.

Agnès caught Artemis's glance. "Needle-work," she said. "Pays tidy. You will be stared at less than in the market. Eyes in the market buy more than coffee."

"I can sew," Artemis answered, and felt the small pride of owning a piece of herself nobody had taken.

"Bon," Agnès said. "But first, church. Otherwise, the ladies will say I brought in a heathen and the neighbourhood will behave accordingly."

They went to St. Augustine on the corner, doors thrown as wide as habit, the pews bought and paid for by families who had traded sugar for absolution. The smell inside was of beeswax and lilies and a hundred damp coats deciding to become dry. Black women in bright headwraps knelt with an economy of motion Artemis envied. White men lowered themselves into purchased pews with entitlement that had learned to pretend humility. Free men of colour stood proud in corners they had made their own, the weight of their hats careful in their respectful hands. The priest came out young and pale and hurried; he spoke Latin as if afraid it might bolt.

Agnès made Artemis dip fingertips in the font, made her cross herself, made her sit without letting exhaustion become spectacle. "Look without staring," she instructed, and Artemis did: at the candles that wrote heat-light above the heads; at a woman who wore grief like a mantle and still sang; at a boy in the back bench who had the oversized ears of someone whose body would one day catch up. She gave the dead their proper minute in her head—sea, aunt, cardman, the Cornishman with competence—then folded the minute away because the living required more change in hand.

After the Ite, they spilled into daylight that talked of Monday. Agnès steered her with a hand at the elbow like a pilot's pole. "Now the market," she said. "You listen to what you do not need."

They crossed Rampart. Voices braided and unbraided. Coffee kettles breathed a sacrament that did not ask a priest's permission. Men with baskets cried fruit in French and then in English, and the same syllables tasted different in each mouth. Calas women sang pastry into being. A fiddler added a penny to the air with each phrase. A man sold lemons as if they would save the city from fever by smelling good alone. Artemis's stomach, traitor turned ally, made its small fists and let them go again. She answered with will and with a cheap biscuit Agnès purchased with an argument so short it must have been family.

A coffee woman, narrow as a spindle and twice as strong, measured Artemis the way weavers measure: for utility. "You pour steady?" she asked, already reaching for a spare tin funnel.

"She pours like a woman counting," Agnès said.

"Half morning," the coffee woman decreed. "Two sous or bread and a seat. You don't drop my cups; you don't flirt. Then go to Riviere and show her your stitches."

Artemis set her hands to work. Pour, turn, wipe, nod, count change—she knew this arithmetic from other rooms. The rhythm laid itself under her skin: eight pours, breathe; six nods, swallow; four cups wiped, look up; two coins, decide. Men spoke over her head with the authority of mouths. Women put down baskets long enough to drink and exchange the gospel that is

domestic war: who had died, who had married badly, who had sent for a cousin and received instead a letter full of weather. The dog, Moss, stationed himself at the stand's rear, taking his wage in heat and observation. When Artemis bent to set down a cup, he leaned his chin against her shin briefly, as if making a note in his ledger: present, serviceable, not owned.

A man paused at the edge of the stand with a look she recognized—river, small crimes, enthusiasm for women as if they were furniture. The hat brim curled river-fashion. His mouth made that lazy hook lawless men learn from other lawless men. He would have been one of those who had watched her fire on the batture. He would have been in the skiff that marked itself away from her chalk. He looked and did not, the way men look when they expect the city to co-sign their appetites.

"Coffee?" Artemis offered, the single word polished to the white of a bone, neither invitation nor refusal.

He looked at her as at a thing he had half owned and misplaced. "Do I know you?"

"No," she said, because sometimes the truth is the angle that costs least.

"Eh." He took his coffee, found it too hot for the mouth he deserved, and left, because the world had placed a better spectacle three doors down. Moss watched him go with the neutrality of a judge who has read the docket and expects a busy afternoon.

By noon her back had learned a discourse about posture; her palms a new intimacy with tin. The coffee woman paid in bread and a small, honest coin. Agnès

kissed the coin like superstition and did not return it; she put it in Artemis's palm with her own hand covering it as if blessing a child. "For luck," she said, but what she meant was *for ownership*.

They went to Madame Riviere's. The door wore a good paint and had learned to close without slamming. Inside, pins made small galaxies in cushions; fabric hung in careful weather; a dress form stood like a woman agreeable and silent. Riviere herself was of a height that permitted authority without climbing. Her hands were quick and her mouth undecorated with lies.

"Show me," she said.

Agnès had brought a square of linen and a needle, the visiting card of working women. Artemis set her breath to the hem: tiny, bloodless stitches, each the same as its neighbour and not resenting it; corners turned as if petitioning and receiving permission; a seam so delicate it might have grown there under a better season. She did not hurry; she did not advertise. Riviere watched with the calm of a midwife, and when Artemis had knotted and bit the thread, she took the linen and held it up to judgment as the morning held a sheet to light.

"You have a hand," Riviere said. "You use your mouth less than you use it. Both are good. Two afternoons this week—one to baste, one to finish. Pay nine sous the day I am satisfied, five if I am not. You will wear a tignon because ladies of different kinds come through my door and I like the door to speak only of thread."

Artemis inclined her head. "I will tie it," she said.

Riviere reached to the shelf and pulled down a square of indigo. "For now. You will buy your own when your hands make coin."

Agnès wrapped the cloth deftly—one-fold, twist, tuck—the city's law from older days turned to fashion. Artemis looked in the small glass and saw a woman not owned by water or chalk or a man; she saw a head her mother would have recognized even from the far bank.

As they left, Riviere added without drama, "If any woman says a charm over you while you work, tell her I pray with pins. It offends fewer people and does the same job."

They laughed—Agnès at the sense of it, Artemis at the world's refusal to become a simple place.

At home, Gabriel heard the coins announce themselves in a cloth fist and said nothing foolish like *congratulations.* He made a level of his hand and said, "Good," the degree of which was both modest and precise. Moss placed his paw on Artemis's foot once and removed it before anyone could accuse him of sentiment.

Afternoon found her on the bench with a scrap and sandpaper again. "Doors," Gabriel resumed. "You'll be making many. Cloth doors, wood doors, doors of speech." He squinted down the edge of a plank the way ship captains squint at a line of sky. "You can live in this city without opening all the doors. Choose your handful and oil their hinges. The others will batter you just to see if you squeak."

"What is the door to the market?" Artemis asked.

"Coffee," he said. "And knowing a stall that will feed you when you cannot pay today."

"And the door to safety?"

He shrugged. "There isn't one. There are doors that open slower."

Agnès, eavesdropping from the washroom because duty requires both clean shirts and clever advice, called, "The door to safety is neighbour women. If you fall, we say you tripped. If you sin, we say the weather did it. If a man bothers you, we sweep our steps with the broom upside down until he remembers his mother."

"Noted," Artemis said gravely.

In the evening, when the light put a coin on every windowsill and the fig breathed green at the back of the yard, a woman came to the fence and put her elbows on it like a cousin. She wore red beads too bright for sorrow and a shawl too plain for vanity.

"You the one the river spit," she said. "I am Delphine. I sell pralines and opinions. You want the first, you get the second for free."

"Bonjour, Delphine," Agnès answered, offering a chair in the air if not with her hands. "This is Miss Danger. She counts."

"I see she does," Delphine said, amused, eyes going quick and kind and then business. "If you want the market's protection, you tell the fish men I said so. If wreckers bother, you tell Police Chief Dayan his cousin would not like to hear who has tried his patience. He has

no cousin, but men believe in cousins more than in saints."

Artemis filed that under *doors built of lies that function like truth* and thanked her without offering change.

Night came pretended polite. The drums from Congo Square lifted—low tonight, Friday's rehearsal for Sunday's answer. It set the boards in the floor to humming at a pitch none of the three of them would confess to hearing. Artemis lay with the knife where knives like to sleep and the cards under her cheek and told her body: *This roof is yours, for now.* Her ribs made one small bell and then another, softer. Moss took the length under the bed and refused, with dignity, to chase a rat that had seniority.

In the deep hour, she woke to the interior weather of fear that arrives even when doors are locked. It asked if she belonged anywhere that walls could recognize. She sat up, quietly, felt the room's edges with her eyes— bench, hanger, window—but did not light a lamp. She pressed her hand to the sternum's second spine and breathed the old way: eight, six, four, two. The panic came to heel like a dog that knows the house's law. She slept.

On the next day she tied the indigo headwrap as Riviere had taught and took her place at a side table with basted seams and a boss who said *bien* when she meant *work faster* and *pas mal* when she meant *you will stay.* A lady came, veiled, smelling of violets and money that had learned to be shy; a woman of colour with gloves too heavy for the weather came with her—maid, companion, cousin, the city's ambiguous algebra. Both looked at Artemis and then learned not to see her. Artemis put her

needle through silk with the patience of someone who knows the difference between being invisible and being spared.

At noon she walked back along doors she had counted and doors she had not, ate bread at the stand where coffee had taught her hands a new clock, and watched two men argue in Irish over whether wages were the correct name for money that never arrived on time. Their vowels knocked against her head like old furniture. She did not introduce herself. Kinship is a binding; she had met enough of those this year.

By late light she had coins enough to buy a kerchief of her own—a cheap cotton with a print that pretended indigo. The woman at the stall wrapped it onto Artemis's head with the correctness of someone tying a sailor's knot: once now; once again; if it comes loose, it is not the cloth's fault. "You walk careful," she told Artemis, and then, because many women are licensed to prophecy if they do it softly: "Don't go after night by yourself; night will not go after you for you."

Evening made a proposal: come as far as the Square and listen from the edge. Agnès allowed it with the frown of an aunt who knows losing would be worse. "Back before the big drum turns the first corner," she said. "That is the rule."

Artemis and the indigo that was and was not hers went as far as the hush before noise becomes itself. Congo Square breathed like a lung that knew the names of a thousand mothers. Drums made a ground under the feet the city did not deserve; songs braided languages together without asking permission. Sticks on bottle, bones, a goat skin made into the instrument that teaches

other instruments to be honest. Women turned, wrapped, signalled to one another with wrists and eyes. Men let spirits ride them or did not, but in either case they danced like beings with gravity's permission. Artemis stayed in threshold's shadow and learned the difference between worship and hunger. She did not step into the circle. She had been inside many circles lately. She had learned to respect their teeth.

Delphine found her at the edge and pretended not to scold. "You stand like someone who remembers nets," she said. "Good. Keep your hips moving anyway; the city reads stillness as weakness."

Artemis let one foot answer the drum. The other refused as an experiment. The drum insisted; the foot amended its vote. She smiled without showing her teeth because joy is its own tether and must be worn carefully.

Home by the law of the house—before the big drum turned the first corner. Gabriel at the bench late—work for a widow who had not asked for a box but would need one tomorrow. Agnès pinning a pattern with authority that forgave no mistake. Moss accepting a crust as if it had requested his permission first.

At the door, Artemis paused, put her palm to the jamb the way Gabriel did, and said the smallest vow: "I will choose the doors."

The house said nothing. Its silence was not a refusal this time. It was the kind of quiet wood makes when it has decided to hold until morning.

"Choose your doors; oil their hinges."

Chapter XVIII — The Work of Breath

*"Keep the count and you can keep a life,
or at least its last hour tidy."*
— Advice from a Charity nurse, 1852

Morning found her at the bench as the law required; the
fig leafed over her like a green hand. Gabriel's plane
talked low; Agnès's broom wrote brisk script across the
boards; Moss made his patrol, editing the street into *ours*
and *not yet*. Tremé answered with kettles and a child's
recalcitrant alphabet shouted over wash. The city had
put on its weekday face: practical, powdered with dust
and flour.

Artemis tied her head in the indigo Riviere had lent and
counted ten breaths on the bench before standing. Ten
for Tremé to see her; ten for her to see Tremé; the old
arithmetic turned domestic. Her body—still a ledger of
small debts—paid interest willingly today. The bruised
place under the sternum where fear kept a thumb had
faded; the knife there had learned to lie flat as a plank.

At the market she poured coffee for men who believed
themselves necessary and women who were. The coffee
woman nodded approval each time Artemis
remembered to set a cup down near fingers that shook.
"You pour like someone who knows the weight of
hands," she observed, which in that parish was
promotion. Moss sat behind the stall with his ledger face
and allowed a toddler to present him a pebble; he
accepted it and returned it and accepted it again, which is
how diplomacy begins.

By midmorning Artemis had earned bread and a coin
and a callus that would hold a needle steadier. She
folded her wages into the hem—pins east, coin at the

seam—and walked the doors she had started to claim: St. Augustine to thank its shade; Madame Riviere's to exchange indigo for work; Delphine's fence for the day's opinion. She did not hurry. Cities smell panic the way dogs do.

Riviere set her at a side table with a ruin of lace that required resurrection. "Madame Duplantier has a ball in five days and her maid has hands like ravens," she said, dry. "You will baste the under-cotton to this ghost so it will live long enough to be worn once with dignity and once more out of spite."

Artemis threaded the needle and found the old surety in the work: small, equal bites; corners negotiated; a seam that did not advertise itself. Riviere watched, satisfied to have hired hands that quieted the air. A client's bell rang; voices—ladies' voices plaited with money—came and went, trailing violet water and the rustle of petticoats that had never earned their starch.

"Where are you from?" one asked in the tone of a person asking the weather to confess.

"Ireland," Artemis said without offering the famine to their table. She kept her mouth thin as a hem and her head low in the etiquette Riviere preferred: a dressmaker sees everything and is noticed by nothing.

"Ah." The woman sighed in a way that forgave no one. "So many."

"So many," Riviere agreed, and shut the door on pity with the efficiency of a well-made hinge.

At noon a boy appeared at Madame Riviere's threshold, cap in hands and knees arguing with each other. "M'selle!" he gasped to the room in general. "Madame Fournier—she's gone bad—can't catch air. Madame Agnès sent me."

Agnès. The cough across the alley had finished being discreet. Riviere's eyes flicked to Artemis's. "You know breath," she said, not asking.

"Yes," Artemis answered, already on her feet. "I count."

"Go," Riviere said, and the indigo square she had lent became a permission rather than a rule. "Bring the count back with you."

They hurried—Artemis and the boy and the dog, who appeared from nowhere as if summoned by the verb *go*. Tremé parted for crisis and then closed again, as a path does after a cart. At the Fournier gate—paint peeling, geraniums stubborn—the air had a smell she recognized from the ship and the swamp and other rooms: a body fighting the world's unkind arithmetic.

Inside, women filled the parlour as they always do in the minutes when doctors are only rumour. Madame Fournier lay on a chaise with a basin near and a rosary in her hand and her lungs making the old, impolite saw. Agnès stood at her shoulder with vinegar and lemon peel and a towel; another neighbour fanned; a third wept decorously by the window as if it were her job.

"Pas trop," Agnès said when the weeper's volume rose. "The dying don't need the noise."

Artemis knelt where the pulse was—at the wrist that had letters inked from other days and the throat where breath performed its small theatre. "We will count," she said, to Madame Fournier and to the room and to herself. "You breathe with me. Eight in; six out; four in; two out. Again. I'll keep the ledger."

Madame Fournier's eyes—startled, then scornful, then a little childlike with terror—fixed on Artemis's mouth. She tried to snatch at air and grabbed only panic. Artemis set her palm against the sternum where a woman carries shame and courage both, light pressure, not consent but companionship. "In," she coached. "Slow."

They made a poor duet and then a better one. Breath agreed half the time; fear made the other half into argument. The room settled around the counting as rooms do when someone has taken sensible authority. The lemon peel's brightness climbed the air. Vinegar scolded; Florida water—Agnès must have fetched it—drew a bright hem around the moment.

A priest arrived, pale and brisk, his cassock hem learning the room's dirt; he stood by the cross for a minute and said words in Latin that had their own discipline; he stepped back when breath required space. A doctor of the city's doubtful middle arrived later, smelling of horse and pharmacy; he set his stethoscope—a wooden trumpet—to the chest and frowned and wrote an instruction that promised very little and then went to the next house where need would write him another page.

Afternoon bled toward evening. Madame Fournier's breath put down its stubbornness and took it up again; panic grew bored with its own performance and dozed; pain, indelicate and honest, remained. Artemis kept

numbers in the air, her voice even as a metronome, her hand a weight small as a coin. Sweat ran at her temples—heat and work—but her gaze did not skate off duty. Agnès caught her eye once and nodded as if at good plane-work.

At last Madame Fournier's hand loosened on the rosary and tightened on Artemis's fingers. "Merci," she said, voice cracked open to the child it had been. "Je... je—" She swallowed, failed, found another path. "Count again."

They did. At some hour that had no number—dark enough for lamps; late enough for men to begin drinking reasons—the breath changed key, the way a song changes when the singer chooses a different door. Agnès moved the towel and the bowl, practical. The priest came when called and finished the Latin; the neighbour women adjusted their weeping to the new grammar: less theatre, more laundry. Gabriel, who had come and not come, stood in the doorway with his hat off in the correct way.

Madame Fournier died the way good women die when the city has not starved their ritual to death: counted, held, seen. Artemis felt the last breath leave, not as a holy wind—she had had enough of winds—but as a household thing: a door closing so the baby won't crawl out.

Someone unpinned the crucifix from the wall and set it on the chest because that is the rule. Someone else tied a scarf under the jaw to persuade the mouth to behave. Agnès pulled the sheet straight with a laundrywoman's correctness. "Tomorrow morning," she said to Gabriel without moving her eyes, "you bring the box. Not the cheap wood. She earned better."

"I know," he said.

Artemis stood, without drama or faint. Her legs agreed to behave as a favour. The room exhaled—relief and disappointment's marriage. The priest nodded once at Artemis's hands without blessing them; he might have, in a different city, but here women have their own bishops.

"Stay to sit," Agnès told Artemis; it was not a suggestion. "We keep her till dawn."

The wake began. Candles made the small, vigilant light. Coffee came, and bread, and caution. Quiet jokes lifted and fell like careful birds; gossip paid its rent even here. Men came to the door and removed their hats and left their opinions outside; women came and stayed, as they always do. A child slept under a chair, his mouth open, the old trust in his throat. Moss lay in the hallway where men would not step on him unless they had never owned a mother.

At midnight, Delphine arrived with pralines and a story about a thief with no imagination; she set both on the sideboard and kissed Agnès's cheek as if that could make the world wash itself. "You," she said to Artemis, not unkind, "sit straight and let your jaw unclench. Death has poor manners but he is not trying to bite you."

Artemis smiled with the mouth only. "He's late to that particular meal."

Delphine approved with a tilt of her head. "You count well," she observed. "When fever pulls the sheet off the city in August, Charity will want you. I will say your name and they will pretend they thought of you themselves."

"Charity?" Artemis asked.

"The big hospital," Agnès answered, mouth a line. "Sisters run it. Men pretend to. You scrub, you count, you bring water, you carry sheets to the dead-cart; you lay a hand to a brow and the house remembers you were there. Coin is coin. Thanks are thanks. Both spend poorly and well."

"Take it," Delphine added, "or take Riviere's coin and thread and let other women die with strangers. We cannot choose all doors. Choose a handful."

A lull in the room's weather brought the sound of drums across the city, quiet, late, private; Congo's own heartbeat answering some other place. Artemis did not close her eyes. She looked at Madame Fournier's neat mouth and thought of Éloise's circle and the chalk that had saved her on the lake and the other chalk that had marked ladders and thresholds. She understood, for the first time without bitterness, that keeping is sometimes love's verb.

Dawn found them unhandsome and true. Men came with shoulders and the right amount of gentleness and lifted the body into the box Gabriel had made—planed in the evening, sanded by candle, corners married as if for love. The lid fitted face-down over the day. Four neighbours took the weight; the priest took the front with his book; women took the back with their opinions and a dish to be returned later with a piece of cake inside because that is how you tell grief: there will be sweetness eventually, just now not for you.

When the house had exhaled silence and scrub water and the last of the lemon peel, Agnès put her palm on

Artemis's cheek. "Eat, then sleep," she said. "You are not a saint. Saints are for pictures. We are for washing."

Artemis ate bread and beans with the gratitude of a sensible stomach. Gabriel poured coffee without speech and set it near her hand and left his hand there for a second longer than habit, an anchor and a question both. Moss tried his trick with the pebble again; she did not return it; he accepted that the game was off today and put his chin on her foot as if to run counterweights for her.

She slept the heavy, punishing sleep that follows work well done and grief only borrowed. Waking came with the city already halfway to noon, bells refusing to mourn unless paid. She washed her face and set her headwrap and tightened her mouth the way a woman does who has decided the next errand without telling the room. At Riviere's, the lace waited without resentment; work makes no room for death's drama after the candles are snuffed. Artemis put needle to cotton, steady, and stitched like someone who had put her hands in a furnace and been permitted to remove them again intact.

In the late afternoon a woman in a dark dress that was not in mourning, not yet, came with an inquiry that had nothing to do with sleeves. Lighter skin than Artemis, hair wrapped not as rule but as fashion, eyes measuring and not unkind. "I am Sister St. Marthe," she said— Creole French in her voice and the small iron certainty of women who do not wait for men to give them keys. "Mother says Madame Delphine stood on a chair at market and told a crowd that a certain Miss Danger can count for the dying. We have need of counters. Can you come three nights and see if your nerves will behave?"

Riviere did not so much nod as not-interfere. "After hours," she said. "She keeps my schedule."

Artemis wiped her hands on the apron and did not ask for time to think. "I can count," she said. "I can carry. I can be quiet."

"Good," Sister St. Marthe answered. "Quiet is the rarest skill." She gave a time and a corner and a door that would not lock from the inside. "Bring vinegar. And a scarf you won't cry over."

When the sister had gone, Riviere set her pins carefully in their cushion as if they were prayers, not tools. "I will not lose you to the sisters full-time," she said, pragmatic as thunder. "I will pay you the day you come back. If you do not, I will speak well of you to your ghost."

Artemis smiled with the level-of-the-plane smile she had learned from Gabriel. "I will come back," she said. She believed it. Belief, lately, had been a currency she had learned not to spend; today she risked a penny.

Evening poured itself over Tremé. Drums spoke in a smaller voice; a cart rolled wrong and then right; a boy laughed with the satisfaction of having stolen an apple in fair fight. Gabriel shaved a plank with the grave content of a man who has decided a day is salvageable; Agnès set vinegar by the door with a bundle of rags and muttered at them for being the wrong size and then forgave them. Moss placed his pebble by Artemis's foot and left it, an offering or a tax.

"Doors," Gabriel said without looking up. "Choose, oil, open, shut."

"I'll oil with vinegar tonight," she said, which made him laugh the way a tired man does—grateful, brief.

At the house on the corner where a fever flag had blown yesterday and been taken in this morning without replacing grief, a woman sat on her step with her head in her hands. Artemis did not sit beside her. She tipped her chin the way the city had taught and kept walking, because sometimes the mercy is bread and sometimes the mercy is letting a person be alone with their door.

She turned her face toward Chartres where Charity Hospital's bulk made the air change temperature. "Count," she told her ribs. "Keep." She touched her knuckles to the jamb as she left the house—Gabriel's habit now hers—and the wood kept his promise without making one. She would stitch; she would pour; she would sit with breath; she would bring water; she would learn which doors to open when the city asked too much. The land had kept her. The city would try. She would keep herself in the remainder.

At the corner, Delphine hailed her with pralines in a brown paper and news not yet needing a priest. "Go on, Danger," she said, amused the way women are when they see themselves repeated in younger, more reckless versions. "Pay your first coin to the sisters. Save the better gold for your own bed."

"I intend to," Artemis said, and stepped into the dusk with vinegar and a scarf she would not cry over and the old, faithful instrument of her chest ready to make numbers into a rope.

"Quiet is the rarest skill."

Chapter XIX — The Night Ward

The hospital had learned to be large. Charity's wings sprawled like a flock that would not be herded, brick and gallery and stair that turned twice when once would do. Lamps burned where day had quit; the air was vinegar and soap and the iron sweetness of blood that had been told to behave. A fever flag snapped on the lee side and then forgot itself. The door Sister St. Marthe named swung inward without complaint, as if it had been oiled for this particular hour.

"Here," the sister said, pressing a square of cloth into Artemis's hand before greetings, before courtesy. "Tie it. Hair stays. Breath stays. Mouth stays shut unless it counts." She was taller at night than she had been in Riviere's doorway, a woman who had lent her daylight bones to darkness and received them back with interest. A thin crucifix lay at her collarbone like a nail in good wood.

Artemis tied. The scarf's knot found its notch. Vinegar in a stone bowl breathed sharp on a table; rags floated, obedient as parishioners. Moss came to the threshold and declined the ward's terms; he sat in the courtyard with the stubborn dignity of a creature who knows when his senses are better used outside.

"Rules," St. Marthe said, already walking. "No promises. They will ask; you will want to. Don't. Water cool, not cold. Rice water if they can keep it down; coffee for the ones who must be kept awake to and through the night. Mouths to wipe. Faces to wash. Sheets to turn. Priest if they ask for priest, never before. Doctor when numbers go wrong. When they die, we make them tidy."

"Tidy," Artemis repeated. The word made domestic sense, and domestic sense kept the dark from setting terms.

"This hall men. Those women. Children down the way because their noise keeps the mothers from dying of silence." The Sister did not slow. "A ledger for breath there; one for pulse. Write fair even if it is for God alone to read."

Artemis took up the chalk. She had worn chalk before—on a deck, in a circle. This chalk did not bind; it remembered. She set the slate against her hip like bread and followed.

The men's ward had been ordered as if order could argue with contagion. Beds in ranks, straw that had been beaten into submission and would revolt by dawn, faces the colour of rinds and the colour of beeswax and the colour men go when the city has learned their names and meant to keep them and then did not. A dockworker with hands like a map mumbled in French for his mother; an Irishman with a chest like a barrel sang two syllables of a psalm and forgot the rest; a Creole clerk clutched a handkerchief as if it held his property deeds. The room hummed with fever's impertinence.

Artemis went to work. Vinegar rag, brow; vinegar rag, wrists. "Eight in, six out," she said to a man who could not afford numbers larger than that. He fought her rhythm, then fell into it because the body, like a mule, finds a step at last. She lifted a cup to a mouth that had been proud yesterday; she refused pride on its behalf

and gave the sip anyway. She wiped mouths without
apology; she turned sheets as if laundering might instruct
a lung to behave. She moved without noise except the
small arithmetic in her throat. Sister St. Marthe flowed
nearby like a draft that knows which rooms deserve air;
another sister, St. Claire, younger and grim with the
terror of doing things rightly, followed with the ledger
and recorded what Artemis marked: respirations
counted in stubborn tens; pulse in four-line columns that
made themselves prayers only out of habit.

"Doctor first?" St. Claire asked at the bed of the clerk
whose nails had turned the blue of mislaid letters.

"Doctor when it matters," St. Marthe answered, reading
the breath as if it were written in print. "This one—later.
That one—now."

The now was a boy so thin he had not yet traded his
voice for hair; a stevedore's son, perhaps, or a baker's
runner, with a fever that made him grander than himself.
"Maman," he said, which is the city's word for all women
when the mouth forgets titles. Artemis placed her hand
on his sternum—a coin, a claim—and kept count out loud
so fear would be embarrassed to interrupt.

A man with shoulders for barrels and a hat he had
forgotten to remove stumbled in the door and stopped
when he saw the beds in their rows. "Seamus?" he said
to the air, the accent turning the name into a tool.
Artemis's eye found no Seamus that would answer. She
stepped toward the man only as far as made him feel
intercepted rather than refused.

"You give the name to Sister at the desk," she said,
keeping her voice where men respond to it and not

where they misunderstand it. "She will read you the ledger. Do not shout. It wakes fever to a worse mood."

The man opened his mouth for argument and closed it. The smell of vinegar and the disciplined light and the rattle of someone else's breath—a neighbour's—corrected him faster than a sermon. He went where she had told him. She had made a door out of a sentence and he had passed through.

A physician came without much ceremony—coat thrown over shirtsleeves, hair gone to grey with no time for drama. Dr. Leclerc, St. Marthe named him under breath. He had an apothecary's nose and the look of a man who had made peace with being contradicted by the sick and by God. He touched two wrists, three foreheads, set a spoon with bark to a tongue that refused and then accepted, wrote a note nobody would read twice, and paused when Artemis said, low, "Breath won't settle at that bed."

Leclerc looked where she pointed as if the pointing had been a rank she had earned. He counted—not aloud, not the way women count, but with two fingers on a pulse and his mouth a line. "Keep him up," he said to Artemis. "If he sleeps, he may forget the trick. You—" to St. Marthe— "cool cloth. You—" to St. Claire— "send for more rice water and none of that night-soil tea the aunties bring. If they insist on offering it, bless them and pour it out the back."

He moved on. Artemis lifted the man as if he were a child too big for sleep; she found how to wedge a pillow so that a rib could remember the angle it had liked before fever took its vote. She spoke numbers, which is the way a body can be told a story without being asked to like the plot.

Down the corridor, women lay in their own grammar of need. A laundress with hands wrung red had come off the line at noon and staggered by dusk; a girl with a new ring clutched it as proof that she had not imagined being chosen; a woman older than accuracy whispered a baby's name into a sheet and the sheet kept it. The children's hall made its argument in bells and sobs. Sister St. Claire, sent to fetch ice that scarcely existed, returned with a small block from a rich house's kitchen, wrapped in flannel and apology; the sisters broke it with the reverence you reserve for relics and laid it at two temples and a throat and watched a fever consider its pride and then decide to postpone its decision by an hour. Hour is grace enough sometimes.

Artemis carried a pail as if it were doctrine. She pared her words back to bone: in, out; sip now; rest; hush. A man with a ribbon on his shirtfront vomited bile and apology; she took both and returned neither. She was not tender; she was exact. The exactness felt like faith. Maybe it was.

At some hour, Lauds for the desperate, a woman with a high collar and a veil that had ideas stood at the end of the ward and did nothing. She was neither Sister nor mourner; money slept in her gloves. Artemis felt the watching rather than saw it. Dr. Leclerc's eye ticked toward the figure and away as if to say: later. Sister St. Marthe noticed and filed the woman under a heading that would matter tomorrow. The watching stayed. The watching, in this city, always does.

Bodies settle by increments if they intend to settle. Two
men did. One did not. He bucked and coughed and tore
at the sheet. The priest arrived, dark as a shut door, and
spoke words that kept their own counsel. Artemis kept
count until the count lost a subject. She laid the hand
straight. She tied the chin. She washed the face in vinegar
and water and mercy until it looked like someone a
mother could recognize. The Doctor nodded at the
result and at her. "You have a hand," he said. In that
parish this was wage and blessing both.

The dead-house took two by the time the lamps burned
low enough to confess they were tired. A cart's wheels
learned the hall and forgot it. Leclerc wrote *phthisis*
once, *yellow fever?* once, *exhaustion* twice, which is the
word men write when they cannot bear the word they
should. Artemis carried a linen bundle as if it were
laundry to the cart and did not flinch when the rope laid
across it was pulled good and snug. She had learned
rope on the Atlantic and in Éloise's yard; rope and she
had a complicated friendship.

"I will take her back," Sister St. Marthe said, when a
young wife's body asked, with its small weight, to be
admitted to dignity. "You sit."

Artemis sat because orders are also doors. Her hands
were vinegar and string. Dr. Leclerc came to the long
table and wrote three names that turned into four,
because one man died while Leclerc was writing.
"Name?" the doctor asked without looking up.

"Danger," she said, and the corner of his mouth
acknowledged the city for its irony. "Artemis."

"Miss Danger." He set his pen down and looked at her properly. "You'll come again. I'll give you a paper if anyone with a hat asks why you're here at hours when men claim ownership of walking."

"A paper," she said, smiling without teeth at the long corridor that had tried to swallow her since Cork. "Useful."

"And a coin," he added, turning the coin with his thumb before setting it under the corner of the ledger as if hiding a blessing from a priest. "The Sisters will scold me if I hand it to you; they think God pays in bread alone."

"God pays in bread," Sister St. Marthe said, appearing with a face that had seen the dead properly to their door, "and I do not refuse coin when it buys soap. Give it her and don't look holy about it."

Leclerc obeyed. Artemis took the coin with a hand that had counted for the living and the dead tonight and found herself steadier because of metal. It did not feed pride. It greased the hinge on tomorrow.

Near dawn, the watching woman returned with her veil in her hand. She was younger than Artemis had first thought, her hair arranged with an expense that had not kept sorrow out. "Sister," she said quietly, "my brother." A name followed, long as a notary's patience. St. Marthe's eyes softened in the way only women achieve: you're late, you're forgiven, sit. The woman sat on the chair the sisters kept for the rich who finally admitted they were not immune. She watched Artemis lay a cool cloth on a brow not much different from her own and did not instruct, or interfere. "You have a—" she began, and then chose the right word. "Method."

"Counting," Artemis said. "It's the only coin I have enough of."

The woman's mouth made a shape not quite smile, not quite ache. "My father owns half a block of Chartres and none of this helps him. If you ever need—" She stopped there because even offers are doors with thresholds that can cut a foot. "Thank you," she finished, which is the city's only honest prayer.

Artemis nodded as if at good joinery. Names were exchanged later—because of course they would be useful another day. For now, the ledger asked for numbers and she had them.

The sky learned pale. Lamps threw up their hands and quit. The ward smelled of sleep and vinegar and a relief that dared not yet pronounce itself. Moss stood at the threshold as if to collect her signature; he sneezed once, which in his language meant *well then*. St. Marthe pressed a crust and cheese into Artemis's hand and the solemn instruction to eat it two doors away, not inside. Leclerc vanished like men do when morning gives them permission to admit fatigue.

Outside, dawn wore small laundry: clouds hung in a row, pinked by the light. The city had not yet remembered to be cruel; it trod water between sins. Artemis ate, standing, because benches were for people who had not found the night's work under their nails. Vinegar dried her hands into paper; she liked the honesty. Moss leaned his shoulder to her shin and bore, for half a minute, an ounce of weight she did not want to carry.

Home had been set to welcome. Agnès had left the pump handle up and a towel and a small bowl of

camphor on the bench under the fig; she had thought of the air before Artemis could. Gabriel had leaned a note in pencil on a board: **Bread on stove. Plane in drawer. Sleep as if you own the house.** It was not poetry. It was better.

Artemis washed like a soldier. She took the bread in two bites, which was reckless, and survived it, which was grace. She set the coin under the oilskin with the Queen and the Tower, and that bit of alchemy—metal beside luck beside warning—made a map in her chest settle.

"You'll go again," Agnès said from the doorway, braid still pinned, eyes like a midwife's dark pan that reflects only what is necessary.

"Yes," Artemis said.

"You'll keep," Gabriel added, the word newly complicated by a city and a sister and a doctor and a ledger.

"For now," Artemis answered, and let fatigue walk her through the law of the house: bench, bed, breath.

She slept through a day's worth of bells. When she woke, the city had moved one name from ledger to ledger without asking her. She tied the indigo without looking. She put her hand on the doorjamb the way men do when they mean to make wood remember them. She counted eight, six, four, two, and found that—astonishingly—numbers can be a kind of courage that never asks for applause.

The night ward waited. So did the market, and Riviere's pins, and Delphine's opinions, and a woman whose veil had been lowered and would be again, and a doctor who had written her name where it would matter to men with hats.

Artemis stepped out. Moss took the street first, because that is the pact. The door closed behind with a small pious click. It would open again.

"Vinegar for hands. Numbers for breath. Mercy for the rest."

Chapter XX — Yellow Days

"Yellow tells you who owes whom."
— From a sexton's pocket ledger, New Orleans, 1852

Heat made a law and then enforced it. By the second
week of June, shutters learned to blink slow; dogs with
any sense slept in the width of a doorway; bread rose
quicker than scripture. Along the levee, flags flared—the
bright, lying blue of ships that wanted attention and, on
certain warehouses and door lintels, that particular
yellow that said *keep away* without bothering to be polite.

Artemis learned the city's summer arithmetic: water,
vinegar, shade; coffee to wake the tired; rice-water to
deceive the sick; counting to keep a grown person from
drowning in the air. Morning at Riviere's table with pins;
midday at the coffee stall with cups; evenings under the
fig sanding wood thin as patience; nights, when Sister St.
Marthe's schedule found her, walking the long corridor
where breath went to be argued with.

"Yellow is the colour of debt," Delphine observed at the
fence, laying pralines out to cool—pecans bellied up in
sugar as if wealth could be taught manners. "It means the
city owes the living care and owes the dead a decent box
and owes the sisters wages they will not be paid."

"And the rich owe God a formula to avoid the fever and
pretend it is piety," Agnès added, not unkind, simply
busy with a shirt that had decided to fight back.

Artemis took the gossip like salt. Outside Riviere's, she
learned other arithmetic—the price of ribbon against the
price of a girl's dignity; the cost of a dress made to be
seen at a ball in August when everyone sensible should
have fled upriver; the coin a woman might pay to look

like someone not marked by last winter's grief. She basted the ghosts of sleeves to bodies that believed themselves permanent and tied her own head neat in indigo that had learned her forehead's measure.

The veiled woman from the ward came not as a spectre now but as a client. She arrived with gloves in June—ridiculous, expensive—and said her name the way old houses say theirs: "Mademoiselle Célestine St. Cyr." Her vowels wore Paris the way other women wore perfume; her ankle showed sense under all that caution.

Riviere's mouth did the thing it did when money entered and pretended to be taste. "Mademoiselle," she said. "We restore lace as well as hem sin."

"I require both," St. Cyr replied, with a small and tired wit. Her eyes found Artemis as if she had known where she would be. "You counted for my brother. He did not die while I was watching, and that seems like something I owe you, even if God will insist on the credit."

Artemis did not look up from the seam she was considering. "Counting is cheap," she said. "I have plenty."

"Not that cheap," St. Cyr said, a coin arriving in a sentence. She slid a card toward Riviere with an address on Chartres and a promise to pay extra for hurry. When the fitting was done—pins bright, muslin murmuring like a well-behaved child—she paused at the door, as if loath to return to a house full of men who made plans and women who cleaned up after them. "If you deliver the bodice Thursday," she said to Riviere, "send Miss Danger. There is a thing beyond stitches we might discuss."

Riviere's eyebrow wrote *mind your schedule and your bones.* Artemis nodded the small *yes* that means *I know doors when I see them.*

On Chartres, the houses had learned their reflection in each other's windows. St. Cyr's wore its shutters like lashes, lowered and raised on command. A black boy with careful hair stood at the door with a cloth in his hand as if he could polish the street into a better neighbourhood. Inside, a maid—young, skin the colour of pecans—took the parcel with gloved hands and a gaze that made no argument about who owned what. Another woman, older, red tignon wrapped high, glanced once at Artemis's headwrap, nodded in the register of women who work for a living, and returned to the business of carrying a tray without spilling dignity.

Célestine St. Cyr received Artemis in a small parlour hung with mirrors that had been bought to flatter and had learned instead to tell the truth by long use. "Sit," she said, which in that house meant not the best chair and not the worst. "You know hospitals. You know markets. You walk in Tremé and you are not owned by anyone I can see." She un-gloved one hand, and her ring sat there like a moral.

"I sew," Artemis answered. "And count."

"Good." St. Cyr crossed a knee. "You will take a piece of lace to a cousin on Rue Dumaine; she pays well and late. You will also carry a message to a man on Royal who prints pamphlets and thinks himself a hero. He is not; he is a shopkeeper with opinions. Tell him that if he will not deliver a certain paper to a certain address on Esplanade, my father will deliver a certain bill to his door."

"Why me?" Artemis asked.

"Because you are not pretty enough to be hunted and not plain enough to be ignored." St. Cyr smiled for the first time; it made her young and then old again. "And because every decent woman keeps a girl who can carry a thing that does not belong to her and return with something of value."

"Will this offend the sisters?" Artemis asked, because doors with hinges sometimes swing onto chapels.

"It will not. It will be done in daylight. It is only business. And if the business smells like politics when you lift its skirt, you will set it down and forget it had a body."

Artemis did not promise. She took the parcel, took the card with its neat hand, took the coin that came honest—wage, not bribe—and left the house with the sense of having stepped through three doors without scuffing the paint.

Outside, she watched an auction—not a grand one with a man on a barrel and a cane tapping the lot number into a back. This was smaller and worse, tucked in an alley's shade: a woman with a child at her skirt, a man with a ledger, two buyers with hats too low, and a priestly sort of silence. The numbers spoken were for bodies, not debts. The child's hand kept finding its way into the woman's pocket, then out, as if to prove a trick learned and useless. Artemis felt her own fingers making fists and opened them.

A man in a blue coat—free man of colour, neat, eyes steady—stood back under the lip of roof and watched, jaw set. He looked at Artemis and knew what she had

learned in the last ten seconds. He did not instruct her to look away. "Keep your face," he said in a voice that had juries in it. "They count that too."

She did. She kept her face and her mouth and her steps. When she could breathe without borrowing the woman's air, she made her deliveries: lace to a cousin whose gratitude came painted; message to a printer with ink on his cuffs and courage on his tongue.

"Tell St. Cyr she is a tyrant and a fine one," the printer said, amused, rolling the paper into its own spine. "Tell her I will deliver, not because she frightened me, but because the words belong to air."

"What is it?" Artemis asked, unable to keep the question in her mouth where good servants put theirs.

"A petition," he said. "A plea dressed as arithmetic. To tidy the quarantine rules. To tidy a city that will not be tidy. It will fail. We deliver it anyway." He looked at her headwrap, at her hands. "You are not a domestique."

"Not today," she said.

"Good." He nodded toward the door. "You will see worse than auctions this summer. If you can leave the room with your face still on, come back here and I will pay you coin to carry words between people who prefer to write their names on other men's spines."

She did not accept. She did not refuse. She took the paper where it needed to go and learned two more back alleys that could lose a woman if a man wanted to.

Fever thinned the city's patience for theatre. In the ward, Dr. Leclerc grew kinder or harsher by inches, but never both at once. "Bathe," he told a dockman who reeked of the river's secret guts. "Or I will send you back to it and tell them you are cured." The man laughed and then obeyed, because laughter is a binding agreement in certain wards. "Write slower," he told St. Claire, who learned to put down a pencil without apologies. "Eat," he told Artemis, handing her the apple he had bitten once and regretted. "You cannot count on spit alone."

Sister St. Marthe's rosary learned her knuckles the way chalk had learned Artemis's palm. "Do not make friends with the dying," she said, setting a bowl of rice-water down where a woman could see it and be persuaded to want it. "It is disrespectful to the living. The world will ask for your whole self; give it a bowl at a time."

Artemis tied a scarf she would not cry over and learned to take small instructions as if they were sacraments. She marked respirations when the doctor's hand had another wrist to hold; she lifted shoulders so lungs could remember upright; she cooled chins and foreheads and the backs of knees and learned there is dignity in the under-known. When a girl no older than Léonie tried to climb the sheet out of panic, Artemis pressed a palm to the sternum and said, "In. Out. Count with me. We will pay this bill."

In daylight hours, yellow made commerce of mercy. A rich man, sleeves rolled perfunctorily, carried buckets for an hour and then spoke of it all week; a poor woman carried buckets all week and then said nothing. The free man in blue—the one with juries in his voice—stood on a corner with a slate and wrote addresses in a tidy hand for those who would otherwise die nameless. "Étienne

Lafon," he told Artemis when she asked for the name a
favour would need later. "Clerk for lawyers who stand
closer to truth than the rest."

"Danger," she replied, and he smiled the way a man
does when introduced to a knife he has been looking
for.

When she and Agnès walked home one dusk with
vinegar and flour, the street presented them with a scene
the city had performed often and never well: a constable
interrupting a row that had not asked for his opinion; a
black woman with a basket and a temper; a boy with
sticky hands and bad timing; a white man declaring the
law in a tone that confessed ignorance of it. Artemis
watched Agnès make a door out of nothing: broom
lifted, mouth composed, head tilted just so. "Officer,"
Agnès said in English flat as a plate, "you don't need to
make work for yourself. This lady would be glad to cross
to the other side before your chief's cousin hears you
raised your voice at someone carrying bread." The man
looked for the cousin who did not exist; the woman
crossed; the boy ran; the scene lost interest in itself.

"Door," Agnès said to Artemis afterward, satisfied and
tired. "Built with lies; still holds."

At Riviere's, Artemis sewed—clean work, thread that
knew when to vanish. In a corner, a girl practicing
stitches confessed a story without meaning to: a brother
in a chain gang digging ditches against the fever's water; a
mother who had once been sold and then had been
bought back in the city by a man with a soft grievance.
Artemis did not look up; she tied a knot neat and bit it
clean; she placed thread in the girl's hand and said, "You

will make fewer knots if you keep your mouth shut while you pull."

They both laughed; it was allowed.

Some business demanded a night outside that was not hospital: a fitting at St. Cyr's, too late because a ball had been moved from Friday to Thursday to make room for a funeral on Friday. Artemis went with the bodice pinned into an argument; Moss trotted at knee, unpersuaded by the city's opinions of dogs in nice streets.

In the St. Cyr parlour she met a man without enough face to be trusted and with the sort of hands that spoke music and also lies: polished cane with a serpent's head; a ring that remembered Paris; an ankle that had learned how to turn toward a woman without being invited. He angled two degrees toward Artemis and then did not pursue the angle, which in New Orleans is called manners. St. Cyr watched him with a sister's resignation. "Monsieur Armand Valade," she said. "He thinks himself interesting."

"Only on Thursdays," he replied with a smile that had made more women complicit than he deserved. "And on days when Miss Danger walks into a room."

He knew her name from a rumour, then. Artemis counted the breaths between his bow and her own neutrally measured nod: eight; six; four. Enough to learn him: a fiddler's wrists, a gambler's attention, a stranger to work who could pretend at it when necessary. He would belong to some later page. She put him down among costs to be calculated.

On the walk back, with the dog alternating between dignified and foolish according to the street's opinions, someone fell in step behind her and then away—a wreckers' gait, remembered from the lake. Moss's low rumble broke it; the footfalls faltered and took a corner that led to less light and more law. Artemis made a door of her own: she cut across the market, passed Delphine's fence where all men behaved, and came home by way of a prayer of wood—Gabriel's doorjamb kissed with her knuckles so the house would remember which body to open to.

"You choose to live?" Gabriel asked, plane stopped mid-song.

"I choose to keep choosing it," she said.

Fever climbed and fell as if it were considering which house to like best. Artemis's nights filled with ledgers; her days with thread. She learned to eat salt before sleep and to drink coffee before counting. She acquired a small procession of thank-yous she did not feel entitled to: bread at a door; a ribbon from a girl whose mother had let her live; a tin medal from a nun who believed overmuch in saints. She kept the medal in the oilskin with the Queen and the Tower and felt, when she lay her cheek to that small reliquary, the map in her chest draws a new line.

On a Sabbath that refused to be restful she followed Agnès to a little service for a laundress dead without fuss, the priest late and the women punctual; afterward they walked past Congo Square, where Sunday had decided to disobey yellow and be itself. Drums stood at a distance from sickness; dance drew circles that kept their teeth to themselves. Artemis did not step in. She had learned the grammar of thresholds. She turned her ear so that rhythm would find her without a net.

Delphine, who understood the mechanics of joy, handed her a praline that was more sugar than sense. "You will make enemies," she warned, not remonstrating, only tidying. "Men don't like women who put numbers in air and make them obey."

"I carry cups and thread," Artemis said.

"You carry breath," Delphine corrected. "It buys more than coffee."

The blue-coated clerk, Étienne Lafon, found her there and tipped his hat as if her name had made him taller. "Miss Danger," he said, with the sobriety of a notary. "If you ever need paper transformed into something that blocks a door, come to me. Otherwise—" He gestured at the circle where women's hips had more theology than any sermon. "Use this."

She smiled without showing teeth. "I'll use both."

Toward month's end, Charity opened a ward just for children, because the other wards' weeping had become imprecise. Sister St. Marthe set Artemis there two nights in a row, the first because she had the hands for it, the second because she didn't flinch when one little boy asked whether he would keep his name if he went where his sister had just gone. "Yes," Artemis said, and meant it beyond doctrine. "Names weigh as much there as here."

"Then I will take ours," he said, and did, which is a sort of mercy and a sort of theft.

When she went home that second dawn, the world had put a clean shirt on and pretended not to smell of vinegar. Gabriel had made a stool for a woman who needed a chair but could afford a stool; he had shaved the edges with care to keep splinters out of a widow's hem. Agnès had a pot on, beans that promised a day not ruined. Moss had acquired a new scar on his ear and acted as if he had been born with it.

"Keep," Gabriel said, handing her a cup.

"I am trying," Artemis answered.

Agnès, practical, set three coins on the table and divided them like a sacrament: one for house; one for thread; one for the poor who would not properly thank you. "And one—" she added, sliding a fourth she must have pinched from somewhere— "for whatever door you knock that I do not approve of."

Artemis kissed her aunt-in-fact's cheek, which is a door you do not need permission to open. "Noted."

She went to Riviere's with fingers that had memorized the weight of small heads and gave them to lace instead. At St. Cyr's she left a bodice that made a woman's sorrow look expensive and took a note to the printer that would shorten no one's fever by an hour and might one day lengthen a poor child's life by a day. In the market she poured coffee with a metronome and scolded a man for pretending his wife couldn't hear the price of sugar. In the evening, she sat under the fig and sanded wood to butter.

Night considered her and found her tiresome. It would try again tomorrow. Artemis washed her hands with

vinegar and camphor and a little soap Agnès saved for Fridays. She lay down with knife flat, cards at cheek, medal in the oilskin between them, and the house doing its polite breathing like a creature who had decided she could stay.

She slept with the new knowledge arranged on the shelf behind her eyes: yellow owed everyone something; thread held as long as pride allowed; men-built doors out of paper and women out of brooms; breath could be kept for an hour if you said the numbers right; and enemies were made by counting in rooms where men had once liked to talk.

She would keep counting. She would keep her face. She would keep, for now, this roof.

"A city keeps what you pay for twice."

Chapter XXI — Faces in the Market

"The market knows more names than the census."
— Proverb of Tremé women, 1850s

By July the market breathed heavier than the river. The heat rose from boards where fish had bled, from baskets where figs softened too fast, from barrels that held water with the reluctance of saints. Men swore in French, Irish, English; women countered with haggling sharp enough to shave coins. Children ran messages that were half errand, half gossip. Every breath smelled of yeast and vinegar.

Artemis poured coffee steady, tin cups shuttling between rough hands and finer ones that trembled no less. "Steady," the coffee woman muttered, approving, when Artemis filled to the lip without spilling. Moss sat under the stall, ledger-faced, tail thumping once only when a child dared touch his ear.

Delphine arrived midmorning, hips proud, pralines rattling in her basket. "Pralines, belles pralines!" she sang, the vowels riding sugar. Then, softer to Artemis: "There's a man with eyes too long on you."

Artemis didn't look. "Which?"

"The one pretending he cares about tobacco price. Black coat, hat curled river-fashion. I saw him at the levee two nights past. Wreckers, most like."

Artemis set down a cup so firmly it stilled on the plank. "Moss saw him."

"And Moss told him, with his teeth," Delphine said. "But wreckers don't stop at teeth." She leaned in, the red

beads at her neck clicking. "Danger, you need neighbours to know your face before the wrong men claim they already do."

As if called, Étienne Lafon—the clerk with his steady slate—appeared at the edge of the stall. "Miss Danger," he said in his notary's careful baritone, "there are men who write names in ledgers that should never touch ink. Better that the market knows yours." He raised his hat. "This is Miss Artemis Danger," he said to the stall at large. "She counts."

The words travelled faster than fish smell. Women looked, measured, and then nodded in the quiet law of markets: *ours, for now.* The wreckers' man lowered his hat brim and moved on, whistling like innocence.

Artemis did not thank Lafon; thanks, makes a leash. Instead, she poured him coffee neat, without coin, and he accepted with the exact politeness of a receipt.

At Riviere's that afternoon, she basted seams with fingers that still smelled faintly of vinegar. The other seamstress-girls whispered while pins clinked:

"They say she sits with the sisters."
"They say she counted a man's breath till he died easy."
"They say she came from the water with no name."

Artemis kept her stitches equal. A hem does not ask to be legend; it asks to hold. Still, she tied the thread with a firmness that might have been pride if pride had not cost so dear.

Riviere, catching the whispers, said briskly, "She sews better than you chatter. Needle speaks truer than gossip." And the room obeyed, because good bosses know when to cut.

Evening under the fig brought neighbours. A boy brought beans in trade for wood shavings Gabriel had given his father to start fires. A girl carried a message from a laundress: *Merci for counting.* Agnès scolded both for bringing shoes into her clean yard and fed them bread anyway.

"You are becoming someone," Gabriel said, planning a board smooth. "Careful which someone."

"What do you mean?" Artemis asked.

"Men will see healer. Women will see hand. Some will see only a name that makes coin." He brushed curls of cypress to the ground. "Choose which face to wear. If you let them choose, you'll be worn through by fall."

Artemis thought of the wreckers' gaze, of Lafon's slate, of Delphine's beads, of Riviere's pins, of St. Cyr's parlour. Too many doors. Too many faces. She pressed her palm flat to the bench as if to keep one thing honest.

Moss padded from the alley; ear nicked fresh. He dropped a piece of cloth at her feet—a torn scrap of black coat, river-stained. She bent, picked it up, smelled smoke and swamp. A message. Or a warning. Or both.

"Rats," Gabriel said, not looking up.

"Not rats," Artemis answered.

That night she tied her kerchief tighter and went with St. Marthe back to the ward. The fever had grown bold, creeping into houses that believed themselves protected by shutters and coin. Children whimpered. Men begged. Women scolded death to its face. Artemis counted, wiped, cooled, lifted. When one woman gasped and whispered, "Tell me I'll keep my name," Artemis said simply, "You will."

The priest came late, muttering Latin. St. Marthe muttered sharper prayers in Creole under her breath. Artemis whispered numbers until breath slowed, then stopped. She laid the jaw, washed the face, and made the body tidy.

When she came out into dawn, the sky was yellow at its edges. Not sickness—just sun, indifferent. She carried the cloth Moss had found in her pocket.

The city was beginning to remember her. The wreckers had not forgotten.

And Artemis had not yet decided which face to wear.

"The market will remember your name, whether you want it to or not."

Chapter XXII — Debts and Doors

"Every coin is two debts: one you pay, one you inherit."
— Saying scratched on a tavern wall, French Market, 1852

The market had learned her name, but names are receipts. By August, Artemis found her days weighed down not only by cups and thread but by errands that smelled of politics and the debts of other people's blood.

Célestine St. Cyr sent her twice in a week: once with a package of lace to a cousin's gallery on Dumaine, once with a folded paper bound in red thread to Étienne Lafon's desk. "He will see it delivered," St. Cyr said, her eyes steady in a way that admitted no refusal.

Lafon accepted the packet with a clerk's solemnity. "Petition again," he explained. "To reform the quarantine laws. Half the city wants the levees closed; half wants them open. All want someone else's house to bear the flag."

"Petition will save no one's lungs," Artemis said.

"No," Lafon agreed. "But it will tell the dead we tried."

He pressed a second folded sheet into her hand. "Take this to the sisters. Quietly. They will know."

Artemis carried both with her coffee wages and Riviere's thread, feeling every alley watch her. At Charity that night, Sister St. Marthe read the sheet once, then tucked it under her scapular without ceremony. "Politics is just another fever," she muttered. "But sometimes it buys vinegar."

In Tremé the yellow flags multiplied. Two doors down from Gabriel's, a cart came at dawn, wheels clattering; a man was carried out wrapped in linen. Agnès swept her gallery three times that morning, hard, as if clean boards could scold contagion. "We will keep vinegar on the steps," she declared. "Anyone tries to carry fever through this door, they will think twice."

Gabriel planed wood for coffins until his hands ached. Artemis helped sand, counting strokes when the silence turned too sharp. Moss patrolled the fence line, bristling whenever strangers lingered too long at the corners.

One evening, Delphine leaned over the fence with pralines and a warning. "Your name is rising too high," she said. "St. Cyr speaks it among her friends. The Sisters speak it in the ward. The wreckers whisper it where they drink. You can't belong to everyone. Decide who pays you."

Artemis broke a praline in half, handed it back. "I'm not for sale."

Delphine laughed, though her eyes did not. "Then you'd better be for barter."

That night, Charity was a furnace. Fever had filled the children's ward; cries braided together until even the sisters bent their heads. Artemis carried water, wiped mouths, steadied small chests with her palm and her numbers. "Eight, six, four, two," she murmured, rocking one girl against her knee until the child's breath settled into reluctant obedience.

Dr. Leclerc moved like a shadow with a ledger. "You keep them calm," he said, glancing once at Artemis's

hand. "Calm saves an hour. Sometimes an hour saves a day." He scrawled *assistant* in the margin beside her name, as if writing her into the ward's bones.

Later, as dawn greyed the gallery windows, Artemis found St. Cyr waiting at the ward door, veil lowered. "You kept my cousin's boy breathing," she said quietly. "You will have coin for that, and protection."

"I did not do it for coin," Artemis said.

"Everything here is coin," St. Cyr answered, eyes sharp. "Even names. Yours is becoming expensive."

Two nights later, leaving the ward with her scarf damp with vinegar, Artemis felt the street shift. A man stepped from shadow—coat torn, the same black cloth Moss had carried home. A wreckers' man, eyes river-dark, mouth ready for lies.

"You're the girl that counts," he said. "Good skill. Shame to waste it on Sisters. Come sit with my captain. He pays better than prayers."

Moss growled low, stepping between. Artemis kept her shoulders square. "I keep who I choose," she said.

The man laughed softly. "Choice is a door, Miss Danger. Doors break."

He faded back into the alley, leaving his words like chalk marks on her ribs.

At home, Gabriel set down his plane when he saw her face. "Who?"

"Wreckers," Artemis said. "They want my count."

"You give it, you'll belong to them forever," Agnès said flatly. "Better to starve."

"Better to sew," Riviere's voice chimed from memory. "Better to sand wood," Gabriel added. "Better to pour coffee," Delphine would have said. "Better to pray," St. Marthe had already muttered.

Artemis washed her hands in vinegar and tied her scarf tighter. "Better to choose," she said to herself, and to the city that was listening.

"Choice is a door. Doors break."

Chapter XXIII — Fever Season

*"In August the city counts in hours,
and even the bells grow hoarse."*
— Note in a sacristan's margin, 1852

August stood on the city's chest and would not get off.
Heat dropped its wet hand on every lintel; shutters
blinked slow as lizards; bread rose in a quarter of the
time and spoiled in half. Yellow flags bred on lintels,
multiplied on warehouses, fluttered on boats like a
coward's parade. Men who had once laughed at caution
tied lemon rinds to their wrists; women sloshed vinegar
on steps until the wood smelled like a scold. The air
tasted of copper and grief.

Charity's wards swelled like riverbanks. Beds that had
learned to be generous ran out of patience. The Sisters
opened two galleries to air and called this merciful; air
came in with mosquitoes and opinions. Dr. Leclerc
moved more quickly by moving less, as if every step had
been measured yesterday and stored against today. Sister
St. Marthe's beads clacked like a metronome; Sister St.
Claire's pencil wore down to nothing and kept writing
anyway.

"Count," St. Marthe told Artemis when speech
threatened to become prayer. "Even when the numbers
disobey."

So, Artemis counted. She kept breath the way a woman
keeps bread dough, turning it, folding it, making it elastic
with hands that understand ordinary miracles. Eight in;
six out; four in; two out. Again. A boy with a scar like
punctuation at his brow learned the rhythm, cursed it,
returned to it like a bad song. An Irish labourer, new-
mouthed and wild-eyed, gripped Artemis's forearm hard

enough to write finger bruises and whispered truths to her he owed a priest; she let them fall to the floor and swept them later into the general account kept by floors. A laundress with a bucket's shoulders wept once, swallowed, and ordered herself to live in Creole sharp enough to make fever consider its manners.

When panic climbed onto a bed and stood there dancing, Artemis pressed a palm to a sternum—coin laid on debt—and made numbers the room's authority. When sleep threatened to drown, she tilted shoulder and pillow, set the body in the old human geometry: ribs like shutters, lungs like small cathedrals. She wiped mouths, cooled knees, tied chins, straightened sheets, set cups to lips that believed cups had been outlawed. She learned how a dying body tries to spit itself back into the living for one last argument. She refused; she accepted; she refused again. Work, repetition, small vows. It is what survives.

Between shifts she sewed and poured and sanded because living pays its rent. Riviere slid harder cloth across her table, work for mornings when minds wanted simple seams. "You have a hand steady enough to offend angels," she said, not quite admiring. "Don't waste it at night." Artemis threaded her needle and did not waste the breath that would argue with a woman who paid in coin and habit. Delphine sold pralines as sacraments; she slid one to Artemis once without charge and said, "Chew. It tells the body its sweet is still possible." Étienne Lafon stood on corners writing names that would otherwise have vanished under bad spelling and worse law.

Célestine St. Cyr sent for Artemis twice in seven days and sent her back out twice more with something folded where only a dangerous woman carries paper. "Deliver this," she instructed, eyes the pale blue of porcelain that will not forgive chips. "To Lafon first. Then to the printer. If anyone asks what you carry, show them your hands."

Artemis carried the paper and cups and thread and the dog's name in her mouth like a coin she could bite to test. Moss took the street first, because that was the pact. Men saw him and hesitated the small half-step that costs a thief his timing.

One afternoon, in the hour when fish stink loudest and men lie most gracefully, a wrecker's man pressed his shadow into hers under the market's awning. Black coat, river brim. The scrap Moss had delivered home gave his sleeve away: mended badly, ash pressed into the cloth as if smoke had been trying to take root.

"You count," he said, conversational as theft. "My captain has a chest that argues like a mule in August. You come and sit. We pay coin that does not ask the sisters first."

"I keep who I choose," she answered, and on *choose* she kept her jaw like a hinge.

He lifted two fingers in salute wide as insult. "Choice," he said. "Nice ornament. Poor door." He drifted off toward the levee where men believed donning river-water made them invisible.

Delphine arrived five breaths later, beads brave as blood. "You keep to the market's side of the street for a week," she advised. "No alleys. No favours after dusk that begin

with 'just here.' Wreckers don't like to beg. It makes them imagine sins they think you owe them."

Agnès agreed with vinegar. "We put it on your collar," she said, dabbing Artemis with camphor like a general with medals. "If a man wishes to put his mouth on you, let his eyes water."

Gabriel kept his counsel and sharpened a chisel. Sometimes a man makes a door by deciding where a wall should end and letting a woman do the rest.

The next night at Charity, Sister St. Marthe turned a page in the ledger with a finger that had learned to be kind without becoming soft and said, "I'll take women. You take children. Men can die without learning manners; babies need instruction." Artemis nodded, tied a scarf she would not cry over, and went where little legs kicked against sheets. She cooled knees. She told a girl with a cough that and did not call it by its church name because naming is not always medicine. She told a boy with a fever he would not keep the name hell had thought for him; he laughed once, high, clean as a new penny; then he slept like an argument lost. When the cart came for the two whom breath had refused to keep, she walked behind it to the door and laid her hand on the board as Leclerc did on a chest: a habit, a respect, not a charm.

Toward dawn, Leclerc leaned on the table and let fatigue give his face an honest ruin. "They won't quarantine the way we need," he said to no one because no one could fix a city with a mouth. "Too much money at the levee. Too much God in the houses with carriages."

"Petitions," Artemis said, and kept her voice from sneering with effort that burned like work.

"They are arithmetic to men who don't like to count," he conceded. He looked at her scarf, at the vinegar dried white at the edges. "I wrote you *assistant*. It will frighten three men with hats and impress two who pay." He slid a folded paper toward her with the look of someone who almost believed in bureaucracy. "If a constable asks what you are doing past ten, wave this like a fan."

She tucked the paper where she kept breath—within reach of hand, within the wall of rib—and took her sleep when sleep permitted: two hours on a pallet whose ticking had learned everything she owned about bones.

When she woke, the city had inched further toward yellow. St. Cyr's cousin had died readable, Riviere said, "and still expects her dress pressed by Thursday," because grief is impatient when it has coin. Artemis delivered the bodice wrapped against heat and looked over the parlour's heads where men spoke politely to each other's vested sins. Armand Valade, with his serpent cane and his hands that could make a bow speak lies, appeared like a rumour you hope to be true and aren't sure about. He bowed a fraction too deep in Artemis's direction to be manners and not yet enough to be insult. "Miss Danger," he said as if trying a note. "I owe Sister St. Marthe two violins for a raffle; perhaps you will remind me."

"I will remind myself," she said, and watched him rearrange interest into something safer.

Out on Chartres, Lafon intercepted her with a slate and a hat and a sentence. "St. Cyr's father will back a quarantine bill if the docks get a special clause," he said dry as law. "Your name is in the paragraph where the sisters are thanked in advance for agreeing."

"They'll deserve it," Artemis said. "Does the bill deserve them?"

"No bill deserves a woman who counts till her voice goes hoarse," he admitted. "But it may buy us three days of closed gates. Three days is a city's breath."

"Three days," she repeated, and tied the number to her ribs.

She went home by the long road men take when they don't want to pass a man they've insulted. Tremé pressed closer in heat's hand. A man with a fever sat on a step counting the boards in his porch rail like rosary; a woman poured water that had learned to be stingy; a child put his face against a barrel's stomach and smiled at the cool wood as if it were a cousin. Moss trotted under the fig and approved passive things—shade, shavings, gravity—over active ones like wreckers and death.

That night wreckers came as promised and pretended to offer hospitality. Two men in a skiff cut close to the bank where the batture makes a grammar of weeds. Moss woke before the wood knew it would creak. Artemis put her hand to the knife she hadn't had to use since the swamp and left it where it lay—the lesson she had learned at Éloise's: a blade is sometimes a letter of introduction and sometimes the wrong language.

The men did not disembark. They whistled once, a river call, and left a wrapped parcel at the water's lip—a length of cloth heavy as ledger paper, a scent of rum, a coin hidden in the fold like a dare. Delphine, who could smell sin two streets over, arrived the next morning and laughed until her beads took offense. "They want you to be their debt," she translated. "You could buy three loaves with that coin and pay for them with sickness for a year."

Agnès threw the parcel back into the river with a washerwoman's contempt. Moss watched it float and did not fetch. The river took it because the river takes everything, good, evil, the wash on Monday. By the end of the week Charity had learned her name the way market had. "Miss Danger," men muttered because Creole mouths liked the rhythm; "Artemis," women said because a first name is what you call a person who has seen your hair unpinned. The children called her *Madam Compte* and *Miss Count* and *the lady with vinegar.* A constable tried once to stop her after dark; she lifted Leclerc's paper and her scarf and her face and he sidled into a shadow that owed him less shame.

St. Cyr sent again. Not a parcel. A carriage. "You will sit with my aunt for an hour," she wrote, not asking. "She believes herself dying. If counted, she may prove herself mistaken, and I will owe you once more in coin or friend." The St. Cyr carriage had opinions, the way wood has when it has been planned by a craftsman and oiled by a servant. Artemis did not like being carried, but the night was hot and the hour small and Charity had not left enough legs in her to walk the length of Rampart twice. The driver flicked the reins like confidence; the yards slid by; a cat waited in a doorway as if for a verdict.

In the aunt's room, lace sighed from mirrors; water sighed in a basin; a woman sighed in a bed without weaving the sigh into more drama than could be afforded. The aunt had the particular chill of a person who had decided to be ill as a preamble to not being ill. "I cannot keep breath," she declared when Artemis set her palm to the sternum that had once known lace better than work. "I am wronged."

"By lungs," Artemis agreed. "They disobey everyone in August." She counted her into a different story. Eight, six, four, two. She cooled wrists. She taught shoulder blades to lie down. She did not scold. St. Cyr watched from the doorway, one hand on the jamb as if holding the house up. When the aunt slept without the jagged theatre she had arrived wearing, Célestine let her shoulders drop half an inch.

"I pay a priest to say words," she said. "He can keep that job. I will pay you to count."

"Pay the sisters," Artemis replied. "Pay Lafon. Pay the printer."

"I do," St. Cyr said, and the smallest smile ruined the veneer at the corner. "But I like to see where a coin lands."

"Then stand in the ward," Artemis said. "Watch a woman with a bucket's hands die sitting up."

"I have stood," Célestine said, and Artemis believed her then. "And I will again."

The carriage left Artemis at the corner as promised, not at the door, because the kind of kindness St. Cyr could afford had its own etiquette. Moss slipped from shadow to shin. He pressed one ounce of weight where the city could not steal it. The fig's leaves lifted their hands in the

slimmest breeze since June. Gabriel had left water by the pump with a lemon slice in it, wasteful, extravagant, necessary. She slept like the honest poor: hard and without ceremony. Woke to Riviere's pins and the market's opinions and Charity's vinegar and drums practicing their Sunday under breath. Woke to Étienne Lafon's slate—a clause passed, a clause amended, a gate closed for thirty-six hours while men cursed the economy and stayed alive long enough to profit tomorrow. Woke to Delphine's laughing scold: "You are becoming a door men want to pass through. Be a door with a lock."

She tied her kerchief and kept the paper Leclerc had given under her palm until it had learned the shape of her hand. She poured coffee for the living and water for the almost; sewed sleeves into shape for arms that would embrace and wring; sanded wood that would be breadboard or coffin side, depending on what the day asked without politeness. She refused wreckers by standing still where the market could see her. She accepted St. Cyr's coin because vinegar costs and so does bread. She paid Agnès first, Riviere second, the sisters third, and tucked one stubborn coin into the oilskin with the Queen and the Tower and the tin saint, and felt the map of herself notch a new street.

In the ward, a girl with a braid reminded her of Léonie and so Artemis did not allow herself to be tender. Tenderness is a leash if you aren't careful with where you tie it. "Count," she told the girl. "And when you run out of numbers, borrow mine." They did. The girl lived to be angry at someone else later, which is a form of health.

On a night when thunder remembered the lake and knocked but did not come in, the wreckers tried one more time. A note under the door, paper with its own stink: Captain needs your hand. Come to the basin at midnight. Bring no dog. It was almost courteous. Artemis burned it over the stove and used the ash to scold a stain on the floor. "I have no more storms for you," she told the air, and meant it. Moss ate a fly and agreed.

September promised nothing and brought less. Still, one morning, just before dawn, the city cooled by a finger-width. Shutters sighed; the air quit being a bully and became only a bore. Charity's breath ledger lightened by two names. Étienne Lafon wrote quarantine extended in a hand that almost counted as joy. Delphine sold out of pralines by noon. Riviere allowed herself to sit down while clients were still in the room. Agnès washed the step with less rage.

"Hold," Gabriel said at the bench, hands flat on wood made honest by planning. "Hold a little more."

Artemis pressed her palm to the jamb the way she always did now and said, "I will." She tied her kerchief; she tucked the paper; she chose the doors; she counted. The city, unwilling and then grudging and then slyly grateful, let her.

The bell at St. Augustine went hoarse at last and rested. Artemis rested her voice while her hands continued. You must save something.

"In fever-time, the hardest arithmetic is who to keep."

Chapter XXIV — Reckonings

"When fever leaves, it counts its change in the coffers of the living."
— Noted in a gravedigger's tally, 1852

By September's end the flags began to drop, one by one. Yellow folded itself from shutters; cart wheels slowed; the bells, exhausted, rang less fiercely. Charity's wards did not empty, but they learned to breathe in longer phrases. Death went quieter, which was sometimes worse: a thief retreating, planning its return.

Artemis felt the change in her hands. Vinegar no longer scalded her palms raw; it dried, left salt, let her fingers remember cloth again. At Riviere's, the muslins and cottons came in lighter shades, mourning seams paused, clients demanding colors as if to insult grief into silence. Riviere's sharp mouth softened a fraction. "We mend for the living again," she said. "For a few months, until the city remembers it can be wicked in other ways."

At the market, the coffee woman spoke briskly again, no longer measuring every customer for pallor. "You pour like you own time now," she told Artemis. "That frightens men worse than fever." Moss settled back to ledger-duty, nose buried in stale bread crusts tossed by children who had been frightened into kindness.

Delphine returned to scolding with sugar. "You kept too many alive," she teased, passing a praline wrapped in paper that bore an oil stain shaped like a saint's halo. "Now they'll want you every season. A woman who gives a city back its dead children? That's no longer a woman, that's an institution."

Artemis only smiled, kept her teeth hidden, and slipped the praline into Agnès's apron when she wasn't looking.

The wreckers did not vanish. They were men who disliked being refused. One evening, Artemis saw them near the levee, black coats hunched, their mouths like knives left on a table. Moss growled low but did not move, as if recognizing that the dog's teeth had already spoken once. Artemis lifted her chin and walked past in full sight of the market, under Delphine's beads, within reach of Lafon's slate. The men didn't step forward. Not yet.

That night, Gabriel shut his shop door early and bolted it, something he seldom did. "Debts," he said, voice low, hands still sawdust-stained. "Theirs. Ours. You can't live in a house that owes too much without cracks."

"I've paid in vinegar and nights," Artemis said.

"Not to them," Agnès countered. "Their coin is obedience."

"Then I'll never pay," Artemis replied, and the firmness in her voice startled even herself.

St. Cyr summoned her again. The parlor smelled of violets and faint smoke. Armand Valade was there, cane twirling, grin easy as a lie. "Miss Danger," he purred, "you've become the talk of two wards and three markets. Tell me—do you belong to the Sisters, or to the streets?"

"Neither," Artemis said evenly. "I belong to my work."

"Then perhaps," St. Cyr said, eyes sharp as scissors, "your work can belong to me. I have friends who require... discretion. Letters carried. Accounts settled. Faces remembered."

Artemis measured the room: Valade's grin, St. Cyr's cool attention, the maid's quiet eyes watching from the hall. "I carry for the sisters," she said carefully. "And for the market. That's enough."

St. Cyr tilted her head, smiled in a way that meant the conversation wasn't over. Valade laughed, twirling his serpent cane. "Danger by name, danger by refusal," he said. "We'll see which debts find you first."

At Charity, Sister St. Marthe placed a hand on Artemis's wrist. "You've lasted a season," she said simply. "Most don't. You've kept more than you've lost. That makes the city owe you."

"I don't want it owing me," Artemis said.

"Too late," the sister replied. "Debts don't ask permission."

Dr. Leclerc scrawled her name again in the margin of a ledger, this time without hesitation. "Assistant. Pay her properly," he ordered. The administrator sniffed and turned a page, but the coin arrived three days later, folded in paper and pressed into her palm. Real wage. Real proof.

She took it home, slid it into the oilskin beside the Queen, the Tower, and the tin saint. When she laid her cheek there that night, the map of her chest felt fuller. Not safe. Not settled. But hers.

Autumn crept into the city: cooler nights, fig leaves dropping one by one, the smell of cane harvest upriver. In Tremé, women swept galleries with less rage, children played louder, men argued in public again without looking over their shoulders for the dead.

But Artemis walked still with her scarf tight, her knife flat under her ribs, her eyes on doors. She had lived through storm, swamp, priestess, fever. She had been prisoner, fugitive, helper, counter. Now the city was teaching her another arithmetic: power.

And power was its own fever.

"When the fever breaks, debts remain."

Chapter Twenty-Five — Measures and Intentions

"Beware the man who counts in compliments.
Music is a ruler, too."
— From a seamstress's sayings, Tremé, 1852

By the time figs had softened and let go of the tree
without argument, the city had learned a slower breath.
Yellow still haunted eaves and stairwells, but it no longer
strutted. Charity's halls kept their vinegar, their ledgers,
their small doctrines—but the nights were not a siege,
only a watch. The coffee woman scolded prices instead
of death. Riviere swapped black ribbons for indigo and
rose, and the girls' heads bent over sleeves with the old
gossip stitched into it: who would wed, who would run,
who would buy their silk in coin that had not been
prayed over first.

Artemis moved among these proofs of survival like
someone who had been granted a lease and meant to
keep it. Mornings at Riviere's table, needle exact;
middays at the market, cups steady; evenings under the
fig at Gabriel's, sanding until wood admitted the idea that
it could be smoother. Moss patrolled as if the city had
hired him and mislaid the paper. Agnès kept vinegar on
the step as a theology that still pleased her.

"You breathe without counting," Gabriel observed one
afternoon, setting his plane and letting it rest there, the
blade bright as a bishop's ring. "Good sign."

"I count for luxury now," Artemis said. "Not for
drowning."

"Keep both," Agnès advised, passing with a basket.
"Husbands and fevers alike return when you least need
them."

They laughed, which is a broom that clears rooms of dread for a whole hour.

The Sisters organized a raffle to fund clean sheets. "We'll sell air to buy soap if we have to," Sister St. Marthe said, and New Orleans, always generous when given a spectacle, agreed to pretend money was virtue for an evening. The promised violins arrived at last with a flourish that smelled of citrus and apology: Armand Valade carrying two cases as lightly as if they were an argument he would win. He bowed to the sisters with a respect that was either genuine or rehearsed to look so; he bowed to Artemis by a degree less, as if their acquaintance had already learned a private grammar.

"You see, Sister," he said, opening one case and letting wood glow in lamplight, "I own a debt even I can measure."

"Own it quieter," St. Marthe returned, though even she slipped a finger along the varnish as if praise could get a blessing past the door.

Valade played because men like him cannot resist rooms; a hymn first, correct and plain, then something that had travelled up from Congo, across from Paris, through a woman's kitchen and a man's thirst. The bow found heat and sorrow for the same audience and did not apologize for either. Artemis, who refused to be fooled by theatre, found her ribcage making room in spite of itself. Music is a counting done sideways. She let it set her breath for the length of two songs and then dismissed it, the way a woman receives a suitor on the gallery and sends him away before the neighbours take notes.

After, in the yard smelling of lamp-oil and orange peel, Valade came to stand at the polite distance men learn in houses where widows have opinions.

"Miss Danger," he said, serpent cane as punctuation, mouth that could make lies behave. "We keep meeting under other people's roofs. I wonder what your door would say if I knocked."

"It would say this house sleeps," Artemis replied. "And keeps its lock."

"Locks are invitations to men with keys," he said, a fraction too amused.

"I prefer doors that remember my hand," she said, and started to go.

"Then let me remember it for you." He moved to block, not touching, an angle of presence. "You count lives. I count measures. Between us we could repair a city."

"Cities don't marry," she said, and his laughter admitted she had drawn blood.

He bowed correctly then, which in this parish is a kind of ceasefire. "Forgive me," he added, sudden and almost plain. "The Sisters are owed. You are owed. If I can pay either debt with my small virtuosity and some tiresome coin, let me." He nodded toward the cases. "I grew up on Rampart. Music kept us when law wouldn't. That is all."

The admission loosened something. He had put a child's street in his sentence. Artemis felt sympathy tug at the seam of her resolve and put a stitch in it, small and neat.

"Then bring milk for the children's ward," she said. "Don't put your name on the jug."

He smiled like a man who suspects he has not been dismissed—only deferred. "As you command," he said, and for once the phrase felt like courtesy and not a pledge extracted.

Work mended days into a serviceable length. Artemis's wages became a line in Leclerc's book and a loaf on the table; Gabriel's plane sang; Agnès's broom lectured; Moss collected pebbles from children and returned them as if training a generation in barter. Étienne Lafon wrote CLAUSE PASSED in tidy chalk on his slate and tipped his hat to Artemis with an impulse that looked like pride; the printer sent her with papers that smelled as dangerous as grief and promised to change less; St. Cyr summoned, paid, withheld gossip as if it were lace.

One afternoon Célestine St. Cyr sent not a note but a dress: a ball bodice to be laced in situ because the maid's hands shook and the mother's nagging would turn fingers into claws. "Come at eight," the message read. "Avoid Royal; crates are being rolled late, like sins. Bring only your pins."

Artemis went because coin is coin and because curiosity is a door women keep ajar. The house on Chartres wore twilight like violet; inside, a chandelier advertised rank like a man's waistcoat. Women in colour—indigo, dove, a green too honest for November—moved through rooms with fans that had read more letters than some men. Men practiced conversation in groups that showed their usefulness to each other. Artemis did what seamstresses do best: she became furniture that moves where needed.

She laced, tightened, soothed, rescued a sleeve from catastrophe; she accepted gratitude that had no idea what to do with itself. In a mirror's corner she caught Étienne Lafon speaking quiet to St. Cyr's father, his slate set aside as if this room were the place where numbers argued with themselves and became *policy*. She caught Valade accepting the attention of three women with the modesty of a man certain of other conquests; she saw him turn away from the brightest of the three when his eye found her at the edge of a door, and she felt the hair at her nape lift—a warning made of pleasure.

On the gallery, breeze at last. The musicians tuned; Valade lifted his bow, and the room stood taller to accommodate a waltz. Célestine came to the threshold beside Artemis and did not look at her. "You chose not to carry my father's paper last week," she said, as if discussing the weather.

"I chose to carry milk instead," Artemis returned.

"Both are necessary," St. Cyr admitted. "Men pretend their papers are milk." She paused. "Valade has good ears and poor pockets. He owes men you do not see."

"I see enough," Artemis said. "I saw him give Sisters their violins when he might have bought his own better boots."

"Even men who owe keep their promises when women are watching," St. Cyr said, turning her fan once as if to lower the night's temperature. "Take him at the worth of his next hour. Never at his last."

She left Artemis with that strange blessing and returned to the room where money rehearsed its kindness.

Artemis felt the weight of the city's new arithmetic on her collarbones and decided to misbehave by an inch: she let the waltz pull her halfway into the doorway, enough to see the couples turn, to feel measure roll under her like a boat that is not dangerous. Valade's bow translated rules into heat. When his eyes found her there, he altered nothing in his arm but a corner of his mouth asked a question. She did not answer it with her face. She allowed one foot to mark time, heel to toe—quiet, precise, hidden by the door.

Later, on the way out with empty hands and a pocket of coins wrapped in Riviere's receipt, Artemis cut across the Square to shorten risk. Rain had cleaned the night and hidden would-be trouble under polite smells. Moss, barred from the St. Cyr doorstep by a footman who did not believe dogs belonged to anyone, waited somewhere near the fence-line, practicing scorn on cats.

She felt the alley bend shift behind her—the small, too-gentle hush of men who beg as a tactic. Two shapes slid out where the lamps failed: black coats, river brims, the mud-soaked economy of men who live in law's lee.

"Miss Danger," one drawled. "We admire your constancy. The captain takes offense at being refused a third time."

Moss stepped out like a verdict; a growl unwound from his chest. The man with the torn sleeve—the one Artemis had smelled of smoke—showed teeth. "Leave the dog. Bring yourself."

Artemis did what Gabriel had taught her and what Agnès had refined: she built a door out of air. "Delphine!" she called, not loud enough to bring a crowd, exactly loud enough to make ghosts of neighbours appear at windows. "Is your cousin—Police Chief Dayan's cousin—not on duty at the corner?"

The wreckers twitched; superstition and rumour cost them a half step. Moss took the inch as an invitation and moved.

A bow-voice cut the alley. "Gentlemen," Valade said, as if greeting patrons after a performance. He leaned on his cane, violin case in the other hand, hat still politely in place. "I've been asked to walk Miss Danger to the edge of Tremé by a woman with more money than mercy. If you'll excuse us."

"Who's asking?" the sleeve-man demanded.

"Every door on Chartres when it decides to open," Valade answered, smiling like a pretty blade. "And three men with ledgers you owe. I can name them, but it will spoil our association."

The wreckers measured him; they measured Moss; they measured the alley's four windows where, now that the city had had its spectacle, faces might be willing to stay. They oiled their absence with a mutter and slid into the night toward less public trouble.

Valade did not offer Artemis his arm. He did not come closer than a gentleman might when he did not yet claim jurisdiction. "Forgive me," he said. "I was coming from a place where waltzes turned men into saints. It ill-suits me to play constable after twelve bars."

"I prefer my constables to be Sisters," Artemis said, breath even, knife flat where it always lay. "Or women with brooms."

"Brooms have more authority than I do," he conceded. "May I accompany you as far as your corner? I promise to let the dog think he is keeping both our lives."

She nodded the small yes that means a city has taught you how to accept a favour without paying interest. They walked three doors' worth in good silence.

"You count," he said at last. "I mark measures. We are both servants of time."

"Time is a poor master," she said. "It keeps no one."

"I've made it keep me, once or twice," he said, almost shy. "Not by begging. By persuading it there was more song."

They came to Agnès's fence. The fig lifted its black hands against the sky. Valade paused at the gate where wood remembered the palms that touched it. He did not reach for Artemis's fingers; he did not drop the format that had kept them decent. He drew a small paper from his pocket, folded around a violet pressed flat by a book's tyranny.

"For your oilskin," he said. "Not a pledge. A... measure, if you have need of one." His smile admitted he had grown up poor and was borrowing from a language he did not own.

Artemis took it because refusing would have been theatre. "Thank you," she said. "Bring the milk."

"I will," he said. "And your door?"

"Keeps," she answered, and meant not only the wood.

He touched his hat brim to her, and to Moss as if acknowledging the city's other constable, and he left, serpent head of cane glancing lamplight.

Inside, Agnès looked up from her mending and saw more than Artemis wanted to speak of. She said only, "Bread's in the oven. Don't let it learn arrogance." Gabriel made a small sound that could have been a plane settling or a man deciding not to say what he had thought.

Alone, Artemis unknotted the oilskin. Queen of Cups—calm to the point of insult. The Tower—bruise at the corner, proud as ever. The tin saint that had come from a sister's palm, crooked and defiant. She added the violet, its scent still alive despite its flattening, and was surprised by the rush of something like hope and its intended twin, fear.

"You don't have to love anyone," she told herself, under her breath, the way you instruct bread. "You have to choose the doors."

She slept with the oilskin under her cheek, the knife like a second sternum, the dog under the pallet, the city doing its version of breathing. Near dawn, she woke to

boards that remembered her weight as theirs now and to a quiet that was not absence but pause.

Later that morning, at Charity, a small jug of milk waited by the steps with no name on it. Sister St. Marthe sniffed, smirked. "Sometimes men obey," she said. "Usually when they think a woman will give them credit." She poured. Children drank. The ledger grew one thin line lighter.

At the market, Delphine shook out her beads and narrowed her eyes. "You let that fiddler walk you," she said. "You'll have to let him stop, too, when it suits you."

"I will," Artemis answered.

Lafon, passing, caught only the last word and approved. "Good."

By evening, the city had made one more inch of room for survival. Riviere paid the girls. Gabriel planed the edge of a coffin, then of a breadboard, and preferred the latter. Agnès put a clean cloth on the table as if it were sacraments without sermon. Moss stole nothing and returned what he had not taken.

Artemis stood at the door and pressed her palm to the jamb. The wood had learned her by now. She counted—not because she was drowning, not because someone else's lungs had written a debt in the air—but because numbers can be a song you sing to yourself when the city is deciding whether to be kind.

Eight, six, four, two. Choose.

The violet lay in the oilskin beside the calm Queen and the ruined Tower, and if it breathed, it did so under her cheek, privately.

Tomorrow there would be work. The Sisters. The market. Riviere. Étienne Lafon's careful letters. Célestine St. Cyr's narrow mercy. Armand Valade's music like a good lie that sometimes told the truth.

The wreckers would remember her refusal and ask again, in the way that all asking becomes law if not answered with a better one. Artemis touched the knife and did not draw it. She touched the door and did not lock it. She touched the oilskin and did not open it again.

"I will be kept only by what I keep," she said into the room. The room took the sentence and made it furniture.

Outside, the drums—small, rehearsal, early for Sunday— found the right heartbeats. Inside, a woman who had been driftwood and net and chalk and fever and bread and vinegar stood on a floor that had agreed to know her. The city, listening as cities do through every guilty keyhole and merciful fence, decided not to answer yet.

To be continued...

"Love is a door that asks for your hand and your hinge."

Epilogue — Cypress Roots

"A city keeps what it cannot bury."
— Tremé saying

Autumn pressed its cooler hand over the city. Figs fell, cane was cut upriver, and shutters swung more freely on their hinges. Tremé's galleries wore their laundry like flags of defiance: shirts and sheets declaring survival, skirts and aprons flaring bright after a season of yellow.

Artemis walked slower these days. Not because her body demanded it—though it did—but because she could afford to. Children waved at Moss as if he were a constable on patrol; women greeted her with nods measured in vinegar and respect. Riviere paid her in coin, not charity. Delphine teased her with pralines and with prophecy. Lafon tipped his hat as if her name had been written on the city's page in ink that could not be erased.

At Charity, the sisters kept their vigil. New faces filled beds, but not in siege. Artemis counted, carried, cooled brows. Not as penance, not as desperation. Simply as work. Her work.

On Chartres, Célestine St. Cyr whispered politics as if it were prayer, sending Artemis with folded sheets that smelled of ink and compromise. In the parlour, Armand Valade drew his bow across strings, smiling as though music might outwit ruin. His glance lingered; a question disguised as charm. Artemis learned to meet it without flinching.

At Gabriel's bench, shavings curled like ribbons on the floor. Agnès's broom muttered approval. Bread rose and

cooled on the table. Moss stretched in doorways that now knew which feet belonged.

Artemis pressed her palm to the doorjamb as she always did. The wood had remembered her hand. She whispered the arithmetic that had carried her across water, through swamp, into ward and market:

Eight. Six. Four. Two.

Numbers were a language. A keeping. A vow.

New Orleans exhaled around her—smoke, bread, rot, hymn, fiddle. A city alive, and unwilling to let her go.

Printed in Dunstable, United Kingdom